Marry Jared Whitewolf?

It was impossible, absurd. So why was she in knots over it?

She looked at her bare fingers. Then she looked around the bedroom with its white furniture and pale blue carpeting. The room looked virginal— probably because it was. No man had ever spent the night in it. She was cautious, and the men she dated were cautious. So what happened to all that great prudence with Jared?

He had discerned her feelings more than any other guy she'd ever dated. He knew she was worried about her thirtieth birthday; he knew she loved babies and wanted her own. If she married Jared, she would have a little baby. Not a year from now, but as soon as they married.

Her thoughts shifted to Jared. His dark eyes and strong arms were as clear as if he was in the room with her. A long, tall cowboy who was all she wasn't. A man who excited her as no other ever had....

Dear Reader,

Welcome to a new year with Silhouette Desire! We begin the year in celebration—it's the 10th Anniversary of MAN OF THE MONTH! And kicking off the festivities is the incomparable Diana Palmer, with January's irresistible hero, Simon Hart, in *Beloved*.

Also launching this month is Desire's series FORTUNE'S CHILDREN: THE BRIDES. So many of you wrote to us that you loved Silhouette's series FORTUNE'S CHILDREN— now here's a whole new branch of the family! Award-winning author Jennifer Greene inaugurates this series with *The Honor Bound Groom*.

Popular Anne Marie Winston begins BUTLER COUNTY BRIDES, a new miniseries about three small-town friends who find true love, with *The Baby Consultant*. Sara Orwig offers us a marriage of convenience in *The Cowboy's Seductive Proposal*. Next, experience love on a ranch in *Hart's Baby* by Christy Lockhart. And opposites attract in *The Scandalous Heiress* by Kathryn Taylor.

So, indulge yourself in 1999 with Silhouette Desire— powerful, provocative and passionate love stories that speak to today's multifaceted woman. Each month we offer you six compelling romances to meet your many moods, with heroines you'll care about and heroes to die for. Silhouette Desire is everything *you* desire in a romance novel.

Enjoy!

Joan Marlow Golan
Senior Editor, Silhouette Desire

Please address questions and book requests to:
Silhouette Reader Service
U.S.: 3010 Walden Ave., P.O. Box 1325, Buffalo, NY 14269
Canadian: P.O. Box 609, Fort Erie, Ont. L2A 5X3

THE COWBOY'S SEDUCTIVE PROPOSAL

SARA ORWIG

SILHOUETTE *Desire*®
Published by Silhouette Books
America's Publisher of Contemporary Romance

SILHOUETTE BOOKS

ISBN 0-373-76192-9

THE COWBOY'S SEDUCTIVE PROPOSAL

Printed in U.S.A.

Books by Sara Orwig

Silhouette Desire

Falcon's Lair #938
The Bride's Choice #1019
A Baby for Mommy #1060
Babes in Arms #1094
Her Torrid Temporary Marriage #1125
The Consummate Cowboy #1164
The Cowboy's Seductive Proposal #1192

Silhouette Intimate Moments

Hide in Plain Sight #679

SARA ORWIG

lives with her husband and children in Oklahoma. She has a patient husband who will take her on research trips anywhere from big cities to old forts. She is an avid collector of Western history books. With a master's degree in English, Sara writes historical romance, mainstream fiction and contemporary romance. Books are beloved treasures that take Sara to magical worlds, and she loves both reading and writing them.

To Hannah Elaine Slater, another little sweetie...

And with thanks through the years to
Dr. Clifton L. Warren

One

Fifteen more minutes of peace. Faith Kolanko glanced at her watch and sighed. She could enjoy her lunch break a little longer before she had to return to her frenzied office at Graphic Design. This was her one chance during the day for solitude.

Even when it was almost uncomfortably warm like today, she loved this secluded area of Harrington Park in downtown Tulsa. In addition to a redbrick wall, a tall hedge of blooming spirea bushes hemmed in the niche where she sat. Higher than her head, the white wall of spirea divided the quiet hideaway from the rest of the park.

"Ah, darlin', isn't this a gorgeous day?"

Beyond the spirea bushes a rich bass voice floated on the air. Figuring the couple would move on, Faith paid little heed to their murmurings. A glance at her watch showed twelve more minutes of tranquillity.

She didn't want to return to the office one minute shy of her hour break. She had worked until ten o'clock last night, and then her day had begun at six this morning. She needed quiet before returning to the Bradley account.

Bushes rustled and noises on the other side of the spirea caught her attention again. She heard the snap of a blanket being shaken and then the pop of a can being opened.

"Lie down there, honey, and look at that blue sky. Can you believe this day?"

Faith sighed. Knowing her solitude had to end, she folded the morning paper, brushed crumbs off her blue skirt, then straightened her blue blouse. The couple on the other side of the bushes sounded as if they were going to stay for a while. She closed her thermos and slipped it into the brown paper bag.

"Oh, darlin', I love you so much! I never would've guessed it possible."

As she listened to the masculine voice that softened with tenderness, Faith's brows arched, and she became aware of the cooings and murmurings on the other side of the bushes. The only way out of this corner of the park was a gravel walk that curved right past the amorous couple. She prayed they would pick up and move, but they sounded pretty comfortable.

"I love you."

Faith heard the whispered baby talk, along with kisses and coos and deep-throated noises. She didn't want to even imagine what was going on. But if the woman began screaming with pleasure, Faith wasn't going to sit quietly. Didn't they know there were people around?

They obviously didn't care, because the noises increased.

Faith frowned at the spilling fountain of white blossoms, the green foliage almost hidden by the spirea blooms. She glanced at her watch. Nine more minutes before she absolutely had to start back to the office. Should she make a loud noise or try to creep past them? It didn't sound as if they would notice her. Or care even if they did notice.

"Honey, wait a minute. There," the man said. "Let's get rid of this dress, darlin' blue eyes. Big, big blue eyes.

Oh, what long lashes you have! You're my precious sweetie...."

What would make perfectly sane adults resort to such ridiculous baby talk? Never in her life had Faith felt inclined to talk in such an absurd manner to any male she had dated. Nor would she ever.

The man's voice faded, replaced by sounds that made Faith blush. She didn't want to hear the noises, but now she certainly didn't want to walk past them. And to get out of her hiding place, she would have to do just that.

She looked at the brick wall and contemplated going over it. The vision of herself in heels and hose and a tight cotton skirt sliding over that wall in front of the busy intersection killed the notion instantly. The only other way to avoid the couple would be to crash through the spirea hedge, and she could just imagine how she would look returning to work with flowers and leaves in her hair.

She glanced at her watch. She had heard about couples having sex in the park, but she had dismissed the rumors as frivolous. All she had ever encountered were other business people and a few transients.

Seven minutes. The gurgles and growls and giggles made her cheeks burn. She debated what to do. Were they stark naked? she wondered.

How many times had her friend Leah warned her that they were too isolated when they came to this spot? Next time she would listen.

"Oh, honey, I love you!" came a whisper. Then more kissing sounds and cooing. "Yum, yum, yum. Take a li'l bite here...."

"For corn's sake!" Faith whispered. She looked at her watch. Five minutes. She bit her lip and frowned. Maybe if she just ran past them, they would never notice her. But could *she* avoid noticing *them?* Sex was not a spectator event.

The sounds became more primitive and garbled, and she

could too easily imagine what might be happening on the other side of the spirea.

"Oh, God! Oh, darlin'!" Unidentifiable sounds she didn't want to hear disturbed the quiet.

Faith wanted to scream. She wanted to yell to them that they were in a very public place and could get arrested for what they were doing. "Get a room!" She silently mouthed the words.

"Darlin', what's the matter?"

In the midst of her mental tirade, Faith realized the man's voice held terror. The woman sounded as if she was gagging. Or having a seizure. The woman might be having an attack of some kind!

"Oh, Lordy, Lordy," the man cried out. "What do I do? What should I do? Merry, darlin', can you breathe? Oh, Lord, help."

He sounded desperate. Faith had CPR training. Knowing she couldn't stand by and ignore someone who was hurt, Faith clamped her jaw, prepared to face two naked lovers, and plunged through the spirea, scattering white petals like a rain shower in springtime.

She spit out spirea blooms and froze in momentary shock, staring into dark brown eyes as a man on his knees looked up at her. Sunlight splashed over broad bronzed shoulders that gleamed with a faint sheen of sweat. Shaggy black hair fell around his face. A muscled chest tapered to a narrow waist.

For one brief moment they stared at each other and then Faith's attention shifted. In his arms he held a baby who was choking. A *baby*. She wore a diaper and a pink ribbon in her tiny black curls, and her little face was screwed up in agony.

"She's choking," the man said, but Faith needed no explanation. The coughing and gasping signaled the baby's distress.

Faith reacted instinctively and with the experience of having dealt with a younger brother, sisters, nieces and nephews. She took the choking baby from him and quickly positioned the child face-down across her lap. With the heel of her free hand, she struck the baby on the back between the shoulder blades. On the second blow, something squishy shot out of the little girl's mouth.

The baby instantly gasped for breath and screamed.

Standing, Faith placed the tyke on her shoulder, patted her back, hugged her close and talked softly to her as she jiggled her gently.

"Thank God!" the man exclaimed. "Oh, thank you, thank you!"

Watching the slender blonde quiet his baby, Jared White-wolf experienced a kaleidoscope of emotions: shock when the woman appeared out of the bushes; terror over Merry's choking; swift relief when the woman cleared Merry's throat of the obstruction. Then his relief transformed into curiosity. Who was the pretty lady covered in white blossoms? Merry was snuggling in the woman's arms, quiet now except for an occasional hiccup.

Jared couldn't have been more dazzled if the sun had dropped halfway to earth. This woman knew how to handle a baby. A bona fide, world-class champion baby handler. Probably a mommy with three kids. His gaze ran down her slender figure, noticing her ringless fingers when she turned her profile to him. Her blond hair, sprinkled with white petals, was fastened with a clip behind her head. A practical watch with a leather strap circled her slender wrist. The blue skirt ended above great knees and long, shapely legs.

Jared stood, wiped his brow and hoped his heart would stop racing. The woman turned to face him.

"Thanks," he said. "That's the biggest scare I've had in years."

"What did you feed her?"

"I gave her a banana."

The woman glanced at the baby in her arms, then frowned at him, and he knew he had blundered. "She's too little unless it's mashed up. You didn't let her have the whole banana, did you?''

"Well, not a whole one, but too damned much," he answered perfunctorily, his thoughts moving on. Merry was twiddling with the woman's silver hoop earring, as blissfully happy now as if the whole incident had never occurred. This golden-haired rescuer really knew how to care for a baby.

He thought of the few disastrous dates he had had since Merry had come into his life. He hadn't met a woman yet who could cope with Merry for more than an hour and never in a crisis. And until today, he had never had a crisis that had been life-threatening.

"She's very pretty," the woman said softly, looking down at Merry. The baby gurgled, smiled and stared at the woman. Jared's pulse jumped.

"You're really good with babies."

"I should be," she said without looking up, and he braced himself to hear she had a house filled with her own. She stopped to smile at Merry, both of them looking beautiful, adorable and contented.

"Why should you be good with them?" he asked, holding his breath.

"I grew up with three younger siblings, as well as an older brother. They are all married now with babies," she answered.

He moved closer, catching a fragrance more enticing than the spring flowers surrounding him. Looking into her wide green eyes, he felt a tension that he recognized instantly and was delighted to discover. The sexual chemistry was icing on the cake.

"Hold still. You have petals in your hair," he said, reaching up to pull white blossoms from the silky waves. His hand brushed her throat, and he felt a tingle that echoed through the emptiness deep inside him.

She reached back to unfasten the clip that held her hair

and gave a shake of her head, scattering petals over her shoulders and onto Merry.

"Here, let me help," he said, watching the woman as he placed his hands on either side of her head. While he looked down into her eyes, he slowly combed his fingers through her soft cascade of golden hair. Green eyes tugged at his senses. She drew a deep breath, and the tension between them sizzled, invisible, yet as tangible as if he had moved close to a blazing fire. Her eyes darkened, and her lips parted slightly as she gazed back steadfastly at him.

Never one for long, deep soul-searching, Jared knew inherently that this woman was special. She had dashed into their lives, and he wanted her to stay.

"I'm Jared Whitewolf," he said quietly, looking at her crystal eyes, flawless skin, full red lips. "You're holding my daughter, Merry—spelled M-E-R-R-Y." His speech was automatic. His thoughts were on her eyes, so cool and filled with a mysterious invitation that revved up parts of him hungry for a woman's touch.

"I'm Faith Kolanko."

"Thanks for coming to our rescue."

"You're welcome."

They stared at each other, and Jared didn't want the moment to end. He didn't feel compelled to talk to break the silence between them because it wasn't an uneasy quiet. Far from it. It was snapping, popping and sizzling with chemistry so hot it should be illegal. While he looked down at her, he saw another flicker in the depths of her eyes.

For the first time since he'd become Merry's father, he momentarily forgot his daughter—forgot everything—except the woman whose wide eyes gazed up at him. Faith Kolanko.

"We're having a picnic. Want to join us?" he asked. "Are you alone?"

"Oh, my soul! I'm late for work!" she exclaimed, glancing at her watch, the magic sparks spinning between them vanishing as if turned off by a switch. "I've got to go," she said, handing Merry to him.

Jared knew a good thing when he saw it, and he wasn't going to let Faith Kolanko slip out of his life ten minutes after she'd arrived in it.

"Hey, wait!" he said, trying to scoop up his boots and shirt and Merry's sundress and hold Merry at the same time.

Faith did not wait. She dashed around the spirea bushes and reappeared in seconds with a purse slung over her shoulder. "See you!"

She ran down the twisting gravel path and vanished beyond a stand of bright yellow forsythia.

"Darlin', we can't let that woman go," he said to Merry, placing her on the quilt he had spread. He yanked on his boots, pulled on his T-shirt. He dropped Merry's pink sundress over her head, straightened it and picked her up to run. He passed the forsythia, sprinting across the grassy park while he looked around, searching for a golden head of hair and a blue blouse and skirt.

Halfway around the park, the brick wall progressively shortened and then ended. There was a parking lot at the north end, and Jared scanned the few people getting in and out of cars for a blue blouse and skirt. He glanced to the east. Beyond the park and the wide expanse of sidewalk, past a fountain with silver water sparkling in the bright sunlight, up wide steps to a tall office building, he spotted fabulous legs, a blue skirt, blue shirt and golden hair. He tightened his grasp of Merry and ran.

Faith Kolanko disappeared through the revolving glass doors of the Harrington Tower. Since he suspected she would be out of sight in an office by the time he reached the revolving doors, he stopped running.

He looked down at Merry, who smiled at him. "You are a sweetie, and I'm sorry I fed you too much banana at once. I won't do that again, I promise," he said, kissing the top of her head. "The lady got away—for now, but not for good. Nosiree. Li'l darlin', we'll get our things and go look for the pretty lady. I'll bet half the men in that building can tell me what office she's in. You liked her, didn't you?''

Merry gurgled and blinked when sunlight splashed over her face.

"Well, so did I. She's special, Merry. I can just feel it down to my bones. Faith Kolanko. That's a pretty name. Merry and Faith. I like that.''

Merry smiled at him, and he settled her against his shoulder as he strode back to the blanket he had spread. He laid her down gently, her big blue eyes watching him solemnly until a bird flitted past, and then her attention shifted to the birds and trees.

Jared folded up their things, finished the can of pop he'd been drinking and put their trash in a nearby bin. He sank down on the quilt, pulled Merry into his arms and got a bottle out of a satchel. "Now, li'l darlin', here's your bottle. You drink up and have a little nap. Then, sweetie, we'll go find the pretty lady we liked so much.''

Jared watched Merry's tiny hands grasp the plastic bottle, and he felt his heart swell with love for this little person he held in his arms. "I'm sorry your real daddy couldn't know you, li'l darlin'. He was a good man and we're not going to forget him.''

Merry's eyes closed, thick black lashes a dusky shadow over her plump rosy cheeks. Jared snuggled her closer, careful not to disturb her as she drank her formula. He brushed a kiss across her forehead. While he watched her drink, he thought about Faith Kolanko. He wanted a date with her. He hadn't had a satisfactory date since Merry had come into his life. And though he had yet to try, he suspected he'd had so few dates that he could count them on the fingers of both hands. He just hoped he couldn't count them on *one* hand.

Whatever the number, it had been too damned few. He liked women and he missed their companionship. But nothing about his life was as simple as it had been before. He had to think about Merry now. He had to be friends with nice ladies who liked Merry and could deal with her. And until today, he hadn't met anyone who fit his criteria—and who fit him.

Faith Kolanko had been marvelous with Merry. She was the first female he had encountered who could really cope in a crisis.

While Merry sucked happily, fantasies danced in his mind. Jared pictured the slender blonde in absolute detail. The way her lips curved in a smile, the hint of curiosity in her green eyes as she looked at him. The cool, decisive way she had taken charge. The warmth she exhibited toward Merry.

He had learned at an early age that a man out in public with a horse or a puppy drew women like honey drew flies. In the last four months, he had learned that a man with a baby also attracted women. Wherever he traveled with Merry—grocery, park, rodeo, beach or mall—women came up to him to see the baby. But when he carried it further, it was different. A man and a woman who met over a horse or a dog could ignore the animal for a few hours. No such luck with a baby. When Merry demanded attention, Jared had discovered that most of the women he encountered either knew little about babies or already knew too much and didn't want anything to do with another one. Romance had gone out of his life almost as swiftly as fatherhood had come into it.

But then, springing forth from a hedge, had come a beautiful lady who obviously loved little babies. "My, oh, my!" he whispered aloud. He looked down at the baby in his arms. She had finished the bottle, and her breath was rapid, rising and falling evenly, telling him she was asleep.

"What a day we've had, eh, li'l darlin'? It will be downhill all the way from here." He placed Merry gently on the blanket. "We're going to get our things and go find the pretty lady. I suspect she isn't going to be able to resist you. We are going to ask Faith to dinner and to become part of our lives. We need her—I can feel it clear down to my toes,'' he said to the sleeping baby.

He paused and looked at the spirea bushes. Only a sprinkling of white petals on the ground indicated that anything had disturbed the flowers. He picked a little sprig and tucked it into the pocket of Merry's bag.

Jared stretched out on the blanket, folding his arms behind his head, and watched white clouds shift across the deep blue sky. He listened to the birds and enjoyed the slight April breeze while leaves caused shadows to dance across him. His thoughts were on Faith Kolanko. She had been calm, cool, efficient. And beautiful. Big green eyes, long legs. In his heart he gave another silent prayer of thanks for Merry's rescue and for Faith Kolanko sweeping into their lives.

All his life, there had been women around—until the last two months. He missed having a woman around. He had thought of marriage—something that had never crossed his mind until he'd become a father. Now he was ready to marry. But now, because of Merry, he couldn't get out and meet women with the ease he had known before. Well, Faith was one lady who had charged into *his* life, and he wanted to keep her there. At least, he wanted her there long enough to see if he wanted her there forever.

Two hours later Jared shook out the soft blanket, rolled it up, then bound it with leather before fastening it to a carrier on his back. Catching his shaggy hair, he fastened it with a leather thong behind his head. Then he carefully placed Merry in her baby carrier and secured her against his heart, brushing her soft hair lightly with his fingers.

"Sweetie, I didn't know how lovable a little baby could be until I met you."

He brushed off his jeans, gathered his things and crossed the park. Whistling, Jared strolled to the Harrington Building and pushed inside. Moments later, he was describing Faith to the receptionist, who shook her head at him.

"I'm sorry, sir. There are a lot of blond women who work in this building."

"Faith Kolanko is about five feet eight inches tall. She has long blond hair, green eyes, a few freckles across her nose—"

"Miss Kolanko works on the fifth floor." A man in a white shirt and dark slacks appeared at Jared's side. "She's an artist and works for Graphic Design."

"Thanks," Jared said, eyeing the man as much as the man was eyeing him. Jared turned, looked at the directory posted near the elevators and spotted Graphic Design listed on the fifth floor.

"We'll have to wait until she gets off work, Merry," he said to the sleeping baby. "We'll come back about four o'clock so we don't miss her."

He strode out into the sunshine and back to the park, this time spreading his blanket in the shade where he could see two of the building's exits.

At four he went to his pickup, where he left the blanket and picnic basket, opting instead for Merry's umbrella stroller. "Now, darlin'," he said, buckling Merry into the seat and handing her a bright blue rattle, "we'll wait for Miss Kolanko to get off work." Hooking Merry's diaper bag over the handle of the stroller, he pushed her toward the Harrington Tower.

They sat in the cool lobby and watched people pour through on their way home from work, but Jared did not spot any tall, beautiful blonde. Five became six, the building emptied, and a security man in a brown uniform appeared.

"Sir, do you work in this building?"

"No, I don't."

"Well, unless you have some reason for being here, I'll have to ask you to leave. I need to lock up the building for the night," he said, switching off some of the lobby lights.

"I'm waiting for Faith Kolanko with Graphic Design."

"Miss Kolanko? Do you mind if I verify that?"

"No, go ahead. I'm Jared Whitewolf," he said, standing.

The security guard crossed the lobby to a phone and placed a call. Jared pushed Merry and the stroller closer.

"Whitewolf. He said he's waiting for you, Miss Kolanko. That's right, a little baby. Yes, ma'am. You're welcome." He replaced the receiver.

"She said to tell you she would be right down. Sorry for the inconvenience, sir, but we have to make the building as secure as possible."

"Sure. I understand. Thanks."

Jared pushed the stroller back to the bench that faced the elevators and sat down to wait, watching as glowing numbers above the elevator moved from five to one. He stood as the double doors slid open and the woman he was going to marry emerged.

Two

Rushed, annoyed that she had to take time to see why the man she met in the park was waiting downstairs, Faith glanced around. Her searching gaze was arrested by a tall cowboy wearing a wide-brimmed black hat with two feathers hanging over the brim, a white T-shirt and a big silver buckle on a hand-tooled leather belt. Jeans hugged his slim hips, and the tips of black boots showed beneath the frayed edges. For an instant she didn't recognize him. The lobby was dim; the hat hid his eyes. And the shaggy black hair she remembered from the afternoon was pulled behind his head, changing his appearance considerably.

The tall cowboy turned a stroller to face her, and she saw Merry Whitewolf. Faith knew the man she was facing was Jared Whitewolf.

"Mr. Whitewolf—"

"Howdy, Faith. And it's Jared. You saved Merry's life, so we're on a very personal basis."

"I have to get back to the office," she said as he approached. She looked down at the baby, who smiled. Faith couldn't resist smiling back. For just an instant the cares of the day fell away. "Hi, Merry," she said, leaning down slightly. "You are the friendliest little girl I have ever seen."

"That's because her daddy's friendly" came a slow drawl. "Sorry to interrupt your work, but we wanted to take you to dinner when you're through here."

"Oh, I'm sorry, I just couldn't!" Faith exclaimed swiftly, straightening to face him. He tilted back his hat, and she looked into dark eyes that seemed to reach down and grab hold of a little part of her soul. She didn't want to look away. She forgot work. She forgot where she was for a moment. In the park today, she had felt that same magnetic pull, but she had blamed it on the sweet baby, the magic of the outdoors on a sunny afternoon, the unusual encounter. And maybe an expanse of a fabulous, bare chest.

She couldn't blame her current reaction on any of those things, yet here she was barely able to get her breath, gazing up at a man who was staring at her as if he had been searching for her all his life.

"Yes, you can," he said quietly, touching a tendril of hair near her face. "You have to eat sometime. Have you already had dinner?"

She felt the faint brush of his warm fingers on her cheek. She knew she looked disheveled. The afternoon had been as hectic as she had expected, and plunging through the spirea bushes earlier had mussed her cotton skirt and blouse. "No, I haven't, but I'm not going to take time now. I have another hour's work to do."

"We'll wait," he said with a smile as he smoothed her collar. When his knuckles brushed her collarbone, she tingled. What was the matter with her? Had she worked until she was senseless? She was reacting to a perfect stranger in a very primitive way.

"No, you shouldn't wait," she argued, making an effort to look away from brown eyes so dark, she felt she was staring into a moonless night. "I can't go out with you. You're a complete stranger. I know nothing about you. And I have to get back to work."

"Faith," he drawled, his hand catching her arm as she started to turn away. His touch was feather light, and she paused, rooted to the spot. "We're not going to stay strangers. Are you engaged or involved with someone?"

"No, but that isn't the point. In this day and age it's dangerous to be friendly to strangers."

"I agree. So let's fix this stranger status." He retrieved a glossy program from his satchel and handed it to her. "Here's my picture. I'm riding in a rodeo at the arena tomorrow night."

She stared at the smiling picture of him and noted the statistics about his bull riding, saddle bronc riding and prizes he had won. "You're a three-time world champion bull rider," she remarked as she read.

With a flash of very white teeth, he grinned. "Somehow, I don't think that's a plus in your book."

"I can't even imagine it," she answered, looking again at his picture. She had to admit the man was not only handsome, he had a charm that was spellbinding.

"You can call out to the arena, and any of the boys will tell you about me. I own a home here in Tulsa. The house is on South Peoria. If Merry could talk, she would verify that I'm safe. And besides that—" he thrust the rodeo program into Faith's hands and pulled out a card from his frayed billfold "—this is my brother Wyatt. He's a detective with the OCPD. We'll go call him and he'll tell you I'm safe. C'mon."

"Oh, no! You don't need to call your brother."

"I'm not going to. *You* are. I have coins here and you can make the call yourself," he said, positioning the stroller in front of Faith while he tugged lightly on her arm. "There's a pay phone, so you'll know this isn't a setup job. You can call the OCPD yourself and talk to Wyatt. He'll tell you I'm totally safe to go out with. If he doesn't convince you, I have another brother, Matt. He's a farmer. Let's start with the cop."

"This is ridiculous. I have work upstairs."

"I know you do and I'm sorry to interfere, but some time tonight you'll have to stop work and go home. And you'll have to eat. Merry and I can help you unwind. Just a little dinner and I'll get you home, so we can start getting to know each other."

"I don't think so," she said, facing him. He was handsome with prominent cheekbones, skin as dark as teak, lashes unbelievably thick, a firm jaw. And every time she received the full force of his dark-eyed stare, she felt weak-kneed and knew she was going to cave in to him. She took a deep breath, trying to summon a *no*.

"Merry really wants you to go with us. She just doesn't know how to say it."

No vanished as he offered the handles of the stroller to her. Faith pushed Merry to the phone. Big blue eyes stared at her.

Jared placed the receiver in her hand, turned her to the phone and put the card in front of her. He plopped a bandanna on the shelf and untied it. Silver coins filled the red cloth. "Now, you just call the OCPD. There's the number. Ask for Wyatt, and then you ask him about my character and reliability."

She turned to him. "I just don't think I have time in my life right now—"

He bent his knees slightly to be at her eye level, then he leaned closer. She caught a soapy scent that was pleasant. "Faith, I think you should," he said quietly. "I think we were meant to know each other. Sooner or later we will. So let's make it sooner."

Her heart started a ridiculous drumming. Never in her life had she had this kind of reaction to a man.

"Call Wyatt," Jared commanded softly.

She turned and began punching numbers. Then she listened as the operator told her the amount of money required. Each coin made a metallic clink. Jared Whitewolf moved away, pushing Merry around in her stroller, and then he hunkered down to talk to the baby.

A deep male voice finally came over the receiver and Faith felt absurd. "Is this Detective Wyatt Whitewolf?"

As soon as he said yes, she launched into an explanation. "This is Faith Kolanko from Tulsa, and I've just met your brother Jared. He's asked me to dinner, and since we're complete strangers—"

She paused as the man at the other end of the line laughed.

"My brother is safe enough," he said, his voice filled with amusement. "With horses and with women he's a will-o'-the-wisp charmer. He's harmless."

"I met him this afternoon, and his little girl, Merry."

The explosion at the other end of the line made Faith hold the phone away from her ear, but she recognized the shock in Wyatt's reaction.

"Let me talk to him," Wyatt said in a tone of voice that had lost all casualness.

Jared must have heard Wyatt's response, too, because he turned and smiled, making her pulse jump. His grin was infectious, softening his masculine features. The man was incredibly appealing.

She held out the phone. "He wants to talk to you."

"I'll only take a second. Do you mind?" he asked, gesturing toward Merry. They switched stroller for receiver, Jared's hand brushing hers ever so lightly, but she was fully aware of the contact.

"Hi, brother. Yeah, I have a little girl."

Faith couldn't help but listen to the one-sided conversation while she wondered what had happened to Merry's mother.

"No. It's a long story, Wyatt. I'll tell you when I see you. Merry's four-and-a-half months old." Another pause, and then he said, "Yeah, it's great."

Jared's voice had softened to a buttery warmth that sent

a tingle dancing in Faith, and she knew he was talking about Merry. His tone changed whenever he talked about the baby.

"I'm riding in a rodeo here tomorrow night, and then we'll be in Oklahoma City for the rodeo next weekend, so we'll come see you then."

He paused and listened. "Yeah, she's with me. How are your girls? And Alexa? Good. Tell them hello. See you Saturday." Jared turned to her. "Faith, do you want to talk to him again?"

She shook her head, then watched as Jared turned back to the phone. With one hand splayed on his hip, he seemed so relaxed, so easygoing, yet there was an air of energy about him that she could feel every time he was near. She would go to dinner with him, she decided. It gave her a peculiar feeling, as if she was caught in a current carrying her along, out of control. Her life was order and stability and security. Filled with routine precision, it was as sure and certain as the hands on a clock. But ever since she had plunged through the spirea bushes and Jared Whitewolf had come into her life, she had felt off balance and out-of-step.

Merry began to fret, and Faith bent down to pick her up. "You have been a very good girl today. You really are a sweetie," she said, remembering that Jared had used the endearment earlier. She turned to find that Jared had replaced the receiver and was sauntering back to her. "Have you been waiting here in the lobby with this baby all day?" she asked.

"No. We spent the afternoon in the park and then came back about closing time."

"Your brother didn't know about Merry."

"No, but he does now. We don't write letters. Now, what do you say about dinner?"

"You'll have to wait around for a little while until I'm ready."

"We don't mind, do we, Merry?" he asked, and Merry smiled at him.

"She's the best behaved baby I have ever seen. She smiles every time anyone looks at her."

"That's because—"

"I know. Because *you* smile a lot," she said, finishing for him as she handed Merry back to him. He grinned while he fell into step beside her and walked with her to the elevator, pushing the empty stroller ahead of him.

"If you'd rather wait in our office, you may. It might be easier with Merry."

"Thanks." He held the elevator door while she entered, and then he pushed the stroller inside. He leaned back against a wall and faced her.

"What's your title?"

"Executive director of advertising."

"I'm impressed. And what do you do? Sell advertising?"

"No. I'm a graphic artist. I plan the layout and design, write copy, sometimes do the entire ad campaign or promotion. I have certain accounts I regularly handle, as well as others I do occasionally, and I have six people I supervise."

While she talked, she was aware of his steady scrutiny. She became more conscious of her appearance, knowing her hair needed combing and her makeup had long ago disappeared. Her blouse was wrinkled and she had a green stain on her collar, probably from the spirea. Jared looked relaxed, one knee slightly bent, his booted foot propped against the wall.

"Do you always work this late?"

"No. We're working on a big account, and the client wanted changes at the last minute, so we're rushing to get everything done. We present the pitch in the morning."

He nodded. "Have any particular food you like to eat?"

"Maybe Italian." She glanced at Merry. "Won't we be keeping the baby up long past her bedtime?"

Jared shook his head. "She sleeps off and on around the clock. And whether she's tucked into her bed or out with us, Merry will sleep. When she's ready to snooze, nothing will stop her. Don't worry, she won't lose sleep," he said, smiling.

"You know best," Faith replied.

The elevator doors opened and she led the way to a glass door that she unlocked.

"You can wait in here."

They entered a large reception area with beige carpeting, dark wood furniture and pots of green plants. Faith turned to him. "I don't know how long I'll be."

He shook his head. "Don't worry about it. We have all the time in the world. At least, until the rodeo tomorrow night."

Feeling the familiar sense of being caught in something she couldn't control, Faith left through a glass door and returned to work. She moved down the hall to a wide table where brochures and folders were spread. Nearby a colorful graph filled the screen of her computer.

Her co-worker and immediate supervisor, Porter Gaston, glanced toward the glassed-in waiting room and his blond brows arched. "Who's your friend?"

"Jared Whitewolf. We're going to dinner later," she tried to say casually, wishing the announcement would go unnoticed, yet knowing it would be as overlooked as a firecracker exploding in a prayer meeting. Without really seeing it, she studied the brochure in front of her.

"You're kidding."

Looking up, she could see the incredulity in Porter's blue eyes.

"Who the hell is he? Where did you meet him?" he demanded.

"He's a friend. Shall we get back to work?" She stared at Porter, feeling a challenge rising. For the first time in her life she was doing something unexpected, unscheduled and uncharacteristic. While Porter looked at the reception area again, she turned to the computer.

"Faith, how long have you known this guy? I know I'm prying, but we're friends."

She turned to face Porter. "I haven't known him long, but I've talked to his brother, who is a detective. Jared is a nice guy."

"Well, damn. I can't believe you're going out with him. Here Madge and I have been trying for two months to get you and Kent together and you're always busy. Yet here in the middle of this project, out of nowhere you're going to dinner with some stranger."

"It's just dinner, Porter."

"How long have you known Whitewolf?"

"His name is *Jared* Whitewolf."

"Sorry. You're evading my question."

"I met him today."

"Good Lord! And now you're going to dinner with that ponytailed cowboy? Faith, the papers are filled with stories about women who get picked up by strangers and the terrible things that happen to them."

"Look, I already told you, his brother is a detective, and I spoke to him. The guy is safe. He seems nice. He has a sweet little baby. He has a house on South Peoria. I read about him riding in the rodeo. I've seen a program with a write-up about him. He's won a lot of rodeo prizes—"

"This is really you talking?"

Annoyed, she turned away. Porter was echoing her own thoughts and causing her regrets to multiply. She didn't know Jared Whitewolf. And even if he was as reliable and charming as his brother indicated, she should be practical and go home to catch up on much-needed rest.

"Sorry," Porter said. "I think I should meet him."

"We will in a minute. Let's finish this up."

She met Porter's quizzical gaze and then he shrugged. "All right. Look at the layout here."

She moved around the table, scrutinizing papers that held graphs and charts and slogans. In minutes she was concentrating on her work again and had returned to the computer, rearranging the information and design. As she moved back to look at a brochure, she glanced through the glass partition.

Jared Whitewolf had tossed aside his hat. He stood with his back to her while he looked at framed pictures of advertising layouts the company had done. Her gaze ran over his thick black hair and his broad chest. The T-shirt molded the sinewy muscles in his shoulders and upper back. His jeans hugged slender hips. He was as foreign to her life as an intergalactic being. And Porter was right. She should tell Jared Whitewolf that she would be working incredibly late and that she would be too exhausted to go anywhere except home. Alone.

She thought of men in her past that she had dated. Without exception, she had known them years before dating them. Buddies, school chums, childhood friends—even Earl Baines, a co-worker whom she had dated the longest. She didn't know anything about cowboys, bull riders or men who spent their afternoons in the park with a baby and wore jeans and T-shirts. She glanced at Porter, who was seated at his desk. He had shed his suit coat, but he still wore his tie and white shirt with well-creased navy slacks. He was the kind of man she knew—professional, ambitious, punctual, whose life was filled with schedules and routines as much as her own.

She would tell Jared Whitewolf goodbye. It was absurd to think of doing anything else.

"Faith, can you look at this?" Porter asked without glancing up. "I think we should move this slogan and the picture of the machinery to the top of the page."

She crossed to his desk and bent over the layout in front of him, forgetting Jared Whitewolf.

It was half an hour later, as she walked back to her computer with papers in hand, that she remembered her date. She glanced toward the reception room, knowing she should put the papers on her desk and send Jared home.

He sat on one of the chairs, and Merry was in his arms

while he gave her a bottle. His head was bent over her, and Faith could see his lips moving and knew he was talking to her. Merry reached up a tiny hand, pale against his dark skin, as her fingers explored his jaw. Something seemed to unfold inside Faith and longing swamped her. She tried to picture Porter holding a baby, giving it a bottle, but it was impossible.

It was equally impossible to imagine either of her brothers—or even her father—tending a baby. With five children, her father had still managed to escape giving one of them a bottle unless he had been settled in front of the late-night news and her mother had placed a baby and a bottle in his arms. Nor could she imagine any of the men she had dated spending the day in the park with a baby like Jared had unless pressed into the duty.

Everyone in her life was as predictable as the sunrise. The men were busy with careers; the women busy with home and children. She was the oldest female and the only unmarried one in her family. Restlessness and a growing dissatisfaction tugged at her while Faith watched Jared Whitewolf. And she decided that this was one night she would spend a couple of hours breaking out of her routine. For once, she would let go of her orderly existence and see what life would be like with someone like Whitewolf.

His head rose and he met her gaze. They stared at each other, and even with a glass partition separating them, her pulse jumped and she felt weak-kneed and fluttery.

She waved the papers at him and he nodded, then she hurried to her alcove to try to finish. They had only the last touches now, and then she and Porter would be ready for the presentation tomorrow morning.

Ten minutes later she looked up to find Porter standing in front of her, gazing down at the brochures and folders and layouts. "We're done!" she exclaimed. "Ten after nine. Not bad."

"It looks great," he said with satisfaction. "Damned good job. I think they'll go for it."

"Thanks," she said, carefully placing the work in stacks.

"I'll wind things up here and then we can go over everything again in the morning before we meet with them. Come on, introduce me to Whitewolf."

She got her purse, shut down her computer and took a last look around.

"You're through, Faith. Stop working."

She smiled at him and they walked to the reception room. Jared came to his feet.

"Porter, this is Jared Whitewolf. Jared, this is my supervisor, Porter Gaston."

"Glad to meet you," Jared said politely, shaking hands with Porter.

"Faith said you're taking her to dinner."

"That's right."

"Before you go, I thought maybe you'd want to look around the office, see some of her work. Faith, why don't you sit with his little baby while I show him our new promotion?"

Hearing the determination in Porter's voice, Faith knew it was useless to protest. And she knew he wanted Jared alone to question him. Porter was a family friend who'd been looking after her for years.

"Now I can see what you've been working on," Jared said easily, and followed Porter beyond the glass door.

Faith felt mildly annoyed at Porter's meddling, but she knew her entire family would be even more curious about Jared Whitewolf than Porter was. She sat down and looked at the baby who was sleeping again, slumped over in the stroller. She looked uncomfortable, so Faith leaned down to unbuckle the strap and carefully lift the sleeping child into her arms. Merry sighed and snuggled against Faith and Faith's arms tightened. She felt a hollow ache while the warmth of the tiny baby seemed to permeate to her heart.

Fifteen minutes later, the men returned and Jared took Merry from her arms. He picked up his hat and set it on his head, and then turned to extend his hand to Porter.

"It was nice to meet you. Thanks for the tour."

"Sure thing. You two have a good evening. I'll wind this up, Faith. If I see anything that isn't ready, I'll give you a call. You don't mind if I call anytime tonight, do you?"

"No. I won't be home for about an hour, but after that, it's fine."

"Good. I might have a question."

"Nice to meet you, Mr. Gaston," Jared said, and pushed open the door for Faith. He wheeled the stroller through the door and walked beside her toward the elevators.

"Sure that wasn't your dad?"

Smiling, she shook her head. "He's a close friend of my father and my uncle, Blake Kolanko. My uncle owns this business."

"Ahh."

"Don't say 'ahh' like 'so that's why you have your job.' I worked at another ad agency until last year when I came to work here."

"I didn't mean any such thing. I just understand better why Gaston was hovering. He didn't want you to go out with me."

"Well, you're not my usual date."

As they waited for the elevator, Jared looked down at her, then touched her collar, his fingers brushing her throat. He stood close enough that she could feel the warmth of his body.

"Who's your usual date?"

"I date men like Porter. They work at brokerage firms or ad agencies. They don't spend the afternoon in the park. And I've known them for years and years." She knew she was rambling, but his brown eyes were playing havoc with her thought processes and she was aware she had worked since six that morning. She smoothed stray tendrils of hair away from her face and wished she had taken more time to freshen up before leaving the office.

He caught her hand and rubbed his thumb lightly across

her knuckles. The touch made her draw a deep breath. Why did the slightest physical contact with him make her tingle?

"I don't see any ring from one of these guys you've known years and years. Who's the one in your life now?"

"Right now, there isn't one. I've been really busy with work for the past couple of months."

He gave her a crooked grin and ran his finger down her cheek. "Sounds like you're ready for a little change in your life."

The elevator doors slid open and he stretched out a long arm, holding the door open while she entered. He pushed the stroller inside.

She looked down at Merry in his arms. "You know, I really don't know you. If it weren't for this baby, I wouldn't be doing this."

Jared stretched out his arm, placing his hand against the wall beside her head and leaned close, bending his knees to look into her eyes. "I didn't have anything to do with your agreeing to go out?" he asked in a husky voice. "You don't feel any little zip of anticipation or curiosity when we talk?"

"Maybe," she answered cautiously, her whole body feeling little zips from his husky voice, his nearness and his question. As she gazed up at him, her breasts tightened and her heart raced.

"Scared to admit it?"

"I told you, this isn't what I'm accustomed to at all. I've never gone out with someone I just met."

"I don't blame you if it's a stranger you don't know. But you know a lot about me. You know I ride in rodeos. You've talked to my brother. And you've saved my daughter from choking. We'll get to know each other better, and tomorrow night you can come watch me ride."

She had to smile. "Too bad you don't have any confidence in yourself," she remarked.

"Faith, darlin'," he drawled, leaning closer and placing his fingers along her cheek, "my confidence is in what I feel and what I see in your green eyes when we stand close like this.''

The elevator doors slid open. As she stepped out and walked through the doors into the night beside Jared Whitewolf, she felt as if she were leaving more than her office and day's work behind.

They placed the stroller in the rear of the pickup and then buckled Merry in the carrier that was in the back seat.

When Jared drove out of the lot, Faith glanced back at the sleeping baby. ''She is the best little baby. What happened to her mother?''

''She didn't want a baby, so she packed and left Merry behind.''

Faith shook her head. ''I'm sorry,'' she said, wondering how badly he had been hurt. ''Having a new baby and losing your wife about the same time must mean huge adjustments. I'm sorry you lost your wife.''

''Oh, I've never been married. I'm not Merry's blood father,'' he answered quietly.

Three

As he drove along darkened streets, Faith stared at him. "You said she's your daughter."

"I adopted Merry when her daddy died," Jared said, his voice rough.

"You must have been close friends," she said.

"He was my best friend." Jared stared straight ahead as he turned into a graveled lot lighted by a tall pole lamp. He parked and cut the motor, still staring out the front window. She saw a muscle knot in his jaw.

"You know, life is strange. My family was such a mess growing up, I finally ran away. I've lived everywhere and done nearly everything, but when Dusty died, it got to me like not much else ever has. I think part of it has to do with Merry. Sometimes when I'm with her, I know what he's missing. It shouldn't be me watching her get her first tooth, it should be Dusty."

"Sorry, Jared. But it's wonderful you took responsibility for her."

"She's my life now," he said, reaching back to touch the baby's wispy hair. "Enough about the past. C'mon, let's eat."

As they stepped out of the car, Faith glanced around. Red neon burned over the door in a simple sign reading Eldon's Café. Across the street was a bar and pool hall, and down the block another bar.

"The area's not great," he said, as if he had noticed her inspection. "But they have the best spaghetti south of Chicago and it's quiet inside so we can talk. You said you like Italian."

"I do. I've lived in Tulsa all my life and I've never eaten here."

"This isn't your style, Faith. Those businessmen you date prefer other places. This is pretty simple," he said as he unbuckled the carrier and lifted it from the rear seat of the pickup. He closed the door and took her arm.

They entered a small, one-room café with wooden tables, an old-fashioned jukebox and men on stools along the bar at the end of the room. A few customers were scattered at booths and tables around the room. Jared led her to a booth and placed the carrier on the seat. He hung his hat on a peg before sitting down to face Faith. As soon as they had glasses of water and had ordered their meals, he took a drink of the beer he had requested and then lowered the bottle to study her.

"Tell me about yourself, Faith. How many brothers and sisters and nieces and nephews do you have?"

"I'm next to the oldest of five siblings. My brothers and sisters are married and all have children."

"So you're the career woman."

She looked down, running her fingers on the cold glass, and watched as little drops of water dripped to the table. "I am. To tell the truth, it's beginning to get a little stale."

"How so? You looked pretty dedicated back there."

"I used to love my work and couldn't wait to get to the office. It was fun and I was eager and it was exciting." She glanced up to meet his steady, disconcerting gaze. "I don't know why I'm telling you all this."

"Because I'm a good listener," he answered lightly. "If you feel that way, why don't you ease up? Go out more. Date. Maybe you're suffering burnout."

"I keep telling myself I don't have burnout, but I don't feel like I used to.... Anyway, now you tell me about you. Two brothers. Where are your parents?" She saw him arch one brow; otherwise, there was no indication she had struck a nerve.

"My parents, darlin', are no longer living. My grandparents are full-blood Kiowa. My brothers and I didn't have the same fathers. Actually, we didn't have any legal fathers—all of them were common-law husbands. My blood father was alcoholic, verbally abusive—not a sterling character."

"I'm sorry," she said, saddened by the knowledge that his past had been so vastly different from her own happy childhood.

He shrugged. "I have two older brothers who are great. Wyatt has grown up with a sense of right and wrong that is powerful."

"Did he get that from your mother?"

"Oh, hell, no." Jared paused as plates of spaghetti with thick red sauce were placed before them. The waitress set a basket with hot, golden breadsticks on the table.

"Can I get you anything else?" she asked.

"No, thanks," Jared answered when Faith shook her head.

"You were telling me about your brother Wyatt," Faith prompted, curious about Jared's family.

"Wyatt got his fine-tuned conviction of what's right and wrong from our granddad. We spent a lot of time on the farm with him. My grandparents live in southern Oklahoma, and they were the Rock of Gibraltar in our lives. We moved all over. I ran away when I was sixteen, so I didn't finish high school," he said, giving her a level look.

"And why do I suspect you have more than one college degree?"

Surprised he had guessed, she shrugged. "I didn't think it showed," she answered lightly. "I have my MBA and a degree in graphic art."

"So our life-styles and our backgrounds are different," he said, putting his fork down. He leaned across the table, sliding his hand behind her head.

She inhaled, his touch bringing a tingling awareness to her whole body. Her pulse raced, and she felt as if she was drowning in his dark eyes. "You have a fancy executive job while I drift across the country riding horses and bulls. Even with all these glaring differences, why do I suspect we have some very common ground between us?"

"I don't think we do have any common ground," she whispered, barely able to get her voice. He was like a magnet, stirring and pulling everything to him.

He leaned back and placed her barrette on the table. "I like your hair better that way," he said.

She touched her hair in surprise. "I didn't even feel you take that out."

Amusement sparkled in his eyes. "I have a practiced hand," he drawled. "A very sensitive touch." She suspected he was not talking about taking out barrettes, but she had never been into light flirting and double entendres, so she let the remarks drop.

"I'll tell you some common ground," he continued cheerfully. "You like Merry, and from the way you look at her, you like little babies a whole damn lot."

"Yes, I do," she said, trying to gather her wits and pick up the thread of his conversation.

"Tell me more about yourself. What do you want out of life?"

She couldn't recall the last time anyone had asked her that question. Or if anyone ever had asked her. She paused, her fork halting. "When I was a little girl, I collected dolls, and all I wanted was to grow up, get married and have babies. Then I got older and began to want a successful career in graphic art. End of ambitions.''

"You want to own the company?''

"Actually, no. I like doing the design and art work. I'm not as interested in management.''

He smiled, a slight curving of his mouth, a satisfied glint in his eyes that made her uneasy, as if she had just passed a test.

"So tell me about your parents and how you spend holidays and where all these siblings live.''

"They all live here in Tulsa, very close to our folks and one another. We spend holidays together, and with all the little nieces and nephews it's fun and hectic.''

Jared finished his dinner and listened to her describe her banker father, her attorney brother, Andy, her stockbroker brother, Keith, as well as her two married sisters who were home with their children. While Faith finished her spaghetti and talked, Jared felt more sure by the second that this lady was going to be special in his life. Every time she talked about marriage and babies, she got a wistful note in her voice. She might have a hell of a career, but the woman wanted a baby, and it showed almost as plainly as if she had announced it.

When Merry stirred, he picked her up.

"I'll hold her if she'll let me,'' Faith said, and Jared handed Merry to her. Faith settled Merry in her arms and smiled at the baby. She touched the baby's cheek. "How did you get to know her father?''

"Rodeo. He was into bull riding and saddle broncs just like I am. I knew Merry's mother, too. She was a good-looking woman. Too damn good-looking. She never intended to get pregnant, and when Merry was born, she took off. She never married Dusty, and she told him she didn't want any part of their kid. Some mother,'' he said.

"So how did *you* become father to her? Or would you rather not talk about it?''

"Dusty lost control of his pickup and he was thrown out.

He didn't wear a seat belt and his internal injuries were terrible." Faith sat quietly while silence stretched between them, and she knew he was having another struggle with his emotions.

"Jared, I didn't mean to pry," she said softly, reaching out to cover his hand with hers.

He turned his head away, pinched the bridge of his nose and wiped his eyes. "Sorry. It seems like yesterday. I got to the hospital as fast as I could. Dusty asked me to take Merry. I didn't want to. Hell, I felt inadequate to be a dad. I damned sure didn't have a good role model growing up."

"Sounds as if you did in your grandfather."

"Yeah, I did. Anyway, Dusty was insistent I take Merry because he was dying." Jared met her gaze and looked down at her hand lying over his. He opened his hand, his fingers closing around hers, warm and strong and sure. Why did every little thing with him seem special? This cowboy was playing havoc with her system, and she suspected she was going to remember this day and night forever.

"Dusty begged me to adopt her. When I agreed, he got a lawyer and we signed the papers. Dusty didn't live until morning."

"I'm sorry."

"Yeah," Jared said, staring beyond her as if lost in memories. He gave her hand a squeeze and released her. Picking up his beer, he took a long drink. "Was I lost at first! I'd never been around a little baby in my life. Never held one. She's an angel and she's blessed my life."

"That's wonderful that you adopted her," Faith said. She was amazed he had adapted so well to fatherhood after the vagabond life he must have led.

"Looks like they want to close," he said, gesturing to the empty café. "Let's get out of here. We can talk in the pickup or we can go to my place."

"My stars," she exclaimed, looking at her watch. "It's half past twelve! We've been talking for over two hours."

He gave her a crooked grin. "So we have," he said, with so much satisfaction, she had to laugh.

"Don't tell me you knew we would."

"I didn't say it." He had paid the check long before, and as he slid out of the booth he placed his hat on his head. He took Merry from her and picked up the carrier.

The night breeze was cool when they stepped outside, catching locks of Faith's hair and blowing them across her cheek. Jared fastened Merry's carrier onto the back seat, and said, "She's asleep again. The afternoon in the park must have worn her out even with her little naps." He slid behind the wheel and turned to Faith. "Give me directions."

She did so, and they drove across south Tulsa to Faith's condo, where Jared punched in the code to open black iron gates. Moments later, he stopped in her driveway and cut the motor.

"Want to see where I live?" she asked. She hadn't given thought to whether or not she would invite him in, simply because she hadn't expected to, yet when he'd switched off the motor, the words were out of her mouth before she could take them back.

"Sure. I'll bring Merry," he said, climbing out of the pickup. He reached into the back seat to gather the baby.

They entered Faith's apartment through a small hallway leading into her kitchen. She switched on a light while Jared placed Merry, still in her carrier, on an oval wooden kitchen table and dropped his hat on a chair. The spotless room contained cherry wood cabinets, tile countertops and a pale blue-and-white floor.

"This is nice," he said.

"I'll give you a tour." Hanging her keys and purse on a hook, she motioned to him, leading him through a formal dining area with a fruitwood table and sideboard, the surfaces gleaming. He thought of the tiny fingerprints smudged on the furniture in his hotel room, Merry's diapers and belongings and toys strewn over the room, and his own clutter.

The living area was equally immaculate with Impressionist paintings hanging on the white walls, muted pastel upholstery lending touches of color in the beige-and-white decor and more fruitwood furniture.

"Would you like a glass of tea or pop?" she asked.

"Whatever pleases you suits me just fine."

He followed her into the kitchen again and when she opened the refrigerator door, he quickly pushed it closed. He placed his hands on the refrigerator on either side of her, hemming her in.

Faith's heart jumped and she drew a deep breath as she gazed up at him. He stood close enough that she could see a faint dark stubble on his jaw. His skin was smooth and brown, his eyes pools of midnight. A faint, thin scar ran across his right cheekbone.

"I don't really need something to drink. Go with me to the rodeo tomorrow night. Come watch me ride."

"Jared, dinner was nice—"

When his dark gaze drifted down to her mouth, her refusal died in her throat. Her pulse drummed, and she could see his intention in his eyes. Her body tightened, heated. The magic chemistry that had flamed between them from the first moments burned hotter than ever. She wanted his kiss, wanted his arms around her. Defying all logic and past history, disregarding every sensible thing she knew, she wanted his kisses. He was an unknown quantity, a temptation to discover secrets life had so far withheld from her. She closed her eyes and tilted her face.

Jared's heart thudded. He saw the invitation, knew she was responding to him the moment her words died.

He knew full well they were as different as a flower from the equator and a glacier in the Arctic, yet a sizzling attraction burned between them. She was wonderful with Merry, and since when had he ever held back because of fear of the unknown?

He slid his arm around her narrow waist, feeling the suppleness of her body, and watched her almost visibly melt into his arms. Her scent was a bouquet of spring flowers. Soft and tantalizing like all the rest of her.

Her hands came up to rest gently on his shoulders—a feather touch—yet the contact jolted him straight to his heart. Her eyes opened to watch him. He could see the questions in their cool, green depths, see the willingness, the invitation that made him shake with anticipation.

His mouth covered hers, tasted, sought and found a heated sweetness that shattered barriers he had built up around his heart too many years ago to remember. His arm tightened and his world shifted, and he wondered if it would ever again be the same. This woman was special to him. They barely knew each other, yet he wanted her. Needed her.

He didn't stop to question whether his feelings were right or wrong any more than he had stopped to question his actions at sixteen when he had run into a dark night, leaving family and home behind.

And he'd felt as if he was searching for something all those years, running, drifting, always seeking. In Faith's sweetness and searing kisses, he felt as if he was home. Yet what could he offer her in return? She was accustomed to business types with their methodical planning and driving ambitions, not rough-hewed cowboys who took each day as it came.

While his heart thudded, he fitted her against his body, one arm tightly around her, his other hand tangled in her silky hair. He felt a chance for a future with her, yet was he pushing his dreams too far? She clearly loved little babies and responded to Merry, yet she might never come to love him.

He gave a deep growl in his throat. He was a man of action, not one to spend time debating the wisest course. She felt right in his arms. She was a marvel; her kisses, her warmth were perfection. Even if he was just a cowboy, she was responding to him. She seemed ready for something more in her life, too. *Take a chance,* his heart whispered.

Her slender arms wrapped around his neck and her hips thrust against him. When she trembled and moaned softly, his temperature soared. He wanted her with every inch of his being.

Faith had never known kisses like Jared's, kisses that made years of loneliness fall away. Nor had she ever experienced the dizzying passion that burned into her, igniting responses she didn't know she had. She felt drawn to this enigmatic man. She sensed a desperate need in him that sought fulfillment as much as the empty void she felt in herself.

Her sane, logical, routine world was torn apart in the raging storm of his kisses. Time hung in the balance. For this moment he was all she knew and, for now, all she wanted to know.

His lean, hard body pressed against her, and she felt his arousal. He raised his head and she opened her eyes, dazzled and befuddled. Kisses weren't supposed to be life-changing. And his kisses had ended too swiftly.

She looked up into smoldering dark eyes that caused her heart to thud.

"Ah, Faith," Jared said softly, running his finger along her jaw. "Will you marry me?"

Four

"Marry you?" Faith gazed up at him, uncertain she had heard him correctly.

Reality came crashing in. Startled by his proposal, she shook her head. Her logical way of viewing a problem surfaced. "Marriage is absurd. We don't know each other at all!" She thought about all the times she had dreamed of marriage. In all those fantasies she had always imagined dating someone for a long time, then getting engaged, followed by months of planning for the wedding.

Too aware of the slightest contact with him, she dropped her hands to her sides. Jared still held her firmly, his arms around her waist, even though she wiggled to move away. "We can't marry," she continued. "If I ever marry, I will be wildly in love. I will have dated him for a long time and known him even longer. My family will know him. We'll like the same things, have the same background—"

"That's not what your kisses just told me," Jared whispered, brushing a kiss across her temple that made her pulse jump again.

"How many women have you proposed to?" she snapped, flustered.

"Only one, just now," he said so solemnly it took her breath away.

"We're strangers and we're not in love."

"I need a mother for Merry. I want a woman in my life. I'm ready to settle down, and you're perfect."

She closed her eyes, her mind reeling. "Get a nanny. Get out and date. You can't know that I'm perfect for you."

"Yes, I do," he answered quietly, and with a firmness that made her want to grind her teeth.

"Well, even if all that is so, there's nothing in it for me. I don't want to marry. I don't know you. You're not perfect for my life—far from it. You're so unlike me. By your own admission, you're wild, a drifter, a cowboy. What makes you think you're ready to settle?"

"Merry. Because of her, I know I'm ready to settle. Darlin', I've seen the world and done everything I wanted to as a single guy. That life is done and over. I've grown up."

She wiggled again, and he released her. She moved a few steps away and turned to look at him. He stood with his hands on his hips, waiting, looking patient and satisfied. And so damnably sexy!

"We don't know each other! I don't even know how old you are."

"Twenty-six."

"Oh, my word!" She reeled at his answer. "There! That's reason enough. I'm older than you."

He stepped close again, and her breath caught in her throat. He tilted her face while he shook his head. "In years you may be older, but not in experience. You thought I was older, didn't you?"

"Yes." The word was a whisper because she knew he had won this argument. She looked at the scar across his cheek, the tiny lines that fanned from the corners of his eyes, the knowledge held in his dark eyes, and she knew that of the two of them, anyone would think he was the older. And when he kissed her, she felt like a young, inexperienced girl.

"How old are you?"

"Twenty-nine," she answered grudgingly.

"Ahh, the thirtieth birthday approaches. How soon is it?"

"Six months." She glared at him, because that milestone had been worrying her more and more often.

"Your biological clock is ticking, Faith. Now I've told you what I want and what I'd be getting. Let's talk about what you want and what you'd be getting."

"I want my career and I'd lose it!" She had the feeling she was hanging on the edge of a cliff and slowly slipping into a bottomless chasm. She could feel ground crumbling beneath her grasping fingertips. At the same time, deep inside, she thrummed with an excitement that she tried to ignore.

"I don't think that's what you want at all." He reached behind his head, unfastened the leather thong and shook his head. Black hair swirled around his face, emphasizing his wildness, and the differences in their life-styles. "You've got your career. You've moved up to a lot of responsibility and you like your work, but it's not enough all by itself, is it?"

She didn't like to admit he was right. Those devastating dark eyes could see to her soul.

He placed his hands on her shoulders, the fingers of his right hand twiddling locks of her hair. "You'd get a family. You would have a baby, Faith."

"I can fall in love, marry and have babies, and you know it."

"But you'll be thirty soon, you're not dating anyone, and marriage is not looming on your horizon."

"That doesn't mean it won't be."

"Of course not, but do you really want to keep waiting?

The scenario you mapped out to me means you'll be about thirty-six before any babies of your own come into your life. And life has a way of handing us a lot of surprises. You can't put life in a daily planner.''

"Marriage is forever. I want to be sure. I want to be in love. You said you had several fathers. You don't have a stable background. I do. I want what I grew up having.'' He was making her uncomfortable because he was voicing some of her own doubts. She felt as if she was arguing half with him, half with herself.

"And I want that, too,'' he said solemnly. "I want a home, a wife and my family. I don't want what I grew up experiencing.''

"Well, then propose to a woman you know really well and you love.''

"I need a wife now. And we can get to know each other and love each other later.''

"And if we don't? Wouldn't that be hellish for us and for Merry?''

"Yes, it would be. Faith, I'm offering you a marriage of convenience. It doesn't have to be physical at first. Then if it's really bad, it can be annulled. Let's see if we can live together—''

"Most of the time it's the other way around. Men want to move in together and then maybe marry.'' She noticed that she was the one whose voice was rising while he was calm, collected. The man was dangerous, a threat to her future and her well-being. "This is impossible,'' she said.

"No, it's not. You're ready for a baby. It shows every time you touch Merry.''

"I have nieces and nephews I can take care of nights on end.''

"That's not satisfying you,'' he said quietly, with a persistence that annoyed her because he was right. It wasn't satisfying her. And she longed for a family, for a baby of her own. She turned to look at Merry, who was sleeping blissfully, unaware of the storm swirling around her that might change her life forever.

"My family wouldn't approve of you."

"They sound warm and loving and reasonable. They can't be vastly different from you," he said.

"They want certain things for me. They expect me to marry someone like the guys I've always dated. We don't go to rodeos or farm or ranch. We're city people who go to the symphony and the opera and the ballet. They want someone with a background like mine—"

"Who is going to pick out this husband—you or your family?"

"You know what I'm talking about," she replied impatiently. It was a crazy argument. She'd never done anything impetuous, reckless or unpredictable. Magic kisses and a sexy cowboy weren't reasons to change.

"Is it my heritage?"

"No, but don't you see, that's simply one more difference upon a sea of differences. It's your hair and your boots and your hat and your life-style and your background and your occupation. How many differences do I have to list? The biggest one is that we don't really know each other. How are you going to support a wife? Riding in rodeos?"

"Actually, that's not a bad way. And at some point, I want to buy some land and raise cattle. I know ranching from the years I spent with my granddad."

"I can't live on a ranch or marry someone who doesn't have a nine-to-five job. We're too different. Thanks for dinner and the proposal...and an interesting evening."

He moved closer and her pulse jumped. His arm went around her waist. "What about this? We seem to agree on this in a most delectable way."

Jared's mouth covered hers in a demanding, passionate kiss that she resisted for one-tenth of a second. As his tongue stroked hers, her insides felt as if they'd been turned wrong side out. A wave of heat washed through her, and her knees went weak. She wrapped her arms around his neck, thrust her hips against him and kissed him back. He was risk and danger, as tempting and breathtaking as a roller coaster. When his arms closed around her, why couldn't she remember that she liked safe, predictable men, the sure and the tame?

The kiss ended abruptly, and she wanted to tighten her arms and pull his head back down. Jared watched her as she opened her eyes.

"Lady, you need kissing. You're primed and ready for some real living after missing out for so long. Maybe we've both been waiting for each other." His words were soft-spoken, but they carried a note of conviction that shook her.

"I'll take Merry home." He released Faith, then strolled across the kitchen to retrieve his hat and to pick up Merry in her carrier. At the door he turned to look at Faith. "I'll pick you up tomorrow night about half past six. I'll show you around the barns, introduce you to some of my friends and get you and Merry settled in your box seats. Afterward, we'll eat some of the Southwest's best barbecue. In the meantime, you think over what I asked." He opened the door and left.

A whirlwind had just swept through her life, leaving silence and devastation in its wake. Or more accurately, she'd encountered a tall, lean cowboy who could see too much and was hell-bent on making her take a long look at herself, and her life.

The rumble of the pickup broke the quiet, then faded into the night. She switched off lights and went to her bedroom, her thoughts swirling with images and questions. She thought about Jared's kisses and her body burned, longing tugging at her. The memory was as clear as if Jared was with her now. Why had his kisses been so spectacular? She remembered watching him give Merry her bottle, the look on his face as he watched the tiny baby. His proposal taunted her. *Marry* Jared Whitewolf? It was impossible, absurd, out of the question. So why was she in knots over it?

Maybe she was suffering burnout at work. She looked at her hands, her bare fingers. Why was she so vulnerable to Jared Whitewolf? The whole day held a dreamlike quality, but his kisses were flaming reality, so much she wouldn't have been surprised to see her hair slightly singed. She would never know kisses like that from anyone else.

"That's no reason to marry someone," she said aloud. But suppose the kisses had been as devastating to him? Suppose this was a volatile attraction they'd never found with anyone else? Shaken by the thought, she moved around the room, getting ready for bed while her thoughts raged over his proposal.

And the sweet little baby. A pang of longing so intense it was painful tore at Faith. Jared Whitewolf had discerned her feelings more than any other guy she had ever dated. He knew she was worried about her thirtieth birthday, and he knew she loved babies and wanted her own. His little girl was precious. Maybe the experience of losing his friend and becoming a daddy really had settled him down.

She could not marry a cowboy! Her parents would have apoplexy. A drifter who ran away from home and never finished high school? He was all wrong for her, and she couldn't believe he'd coerced her into another date tomorrow night at the rodeo.

She looked around her bedroom, with its white furniture and pale blue carpeting. The room looked virginal—probably because it was. No man had ever spent the night in it. She had thought she was in love once in college, but the relationship never developed into anything lasting. Other than that, her dating had never become very intimate. She was cautious, and the men she dated were cautious.

So what had happened to all that great prudence with Jared Whitewolf?

Long after she'd gone to bed, Faith lay wide-eyed, staring into the darkness, remembering holding Merry in her arms, giving her a bottle. If she married Jared, she would have a little baby. Not a year from now, but as soon as they married. And yet, what would her folks think of Jared?

That question brought her back to reality, and she closed her eyes, but in minutes, memories of holding Merry in her arms danced in her head. And then her memories shifted to Jared. His dark eyes and strong arms were as clear as if he was in the room with her. A long, tall cowboy who was all she wasn't. And she had to admit, he excited her as no other man ever had.

Less than twenty-four hours later, Faith had met a dozen friendly people and seen more horses and bulls than ever before in her life. She wondered whether she was the only person in the large metal barn who was not wearing Western boots and jeans. Her pulse hummed with excitement and anticipation, and she was acutely aware of the man at her side. Merry was strapped snugly to his chest and seemed to enjoy her surroundings.

"Come on. I'll get you two settled," Jared said, taking her arm to steer her through the barn. As he reached out to open a door, she looked at his blue-and-white Western shirt, which pulled across his broad shoulders. He looked very much the cowboy tonight with his Western attire.

He led her to an empty box, where he sat with her while he buckled Merry into her carrier in the seat between them. Merry played with a bright red plastic car. Absorbed in her own little world, she raised the car to her mouth to chew on it.

"Here's her bag with bottles if she gets fussy. I'd wait out here with you, but I need to get ready."

"That's fine. We'll be all right. Uh, Jared, I couldn't help but notice you're wearing spurs," she said, a fact that had been worrying her.

He stepped over her and sat down in the seat beside her, propping his long leg on his knee. "The rowels are dull—feel them. I'm not going to hurt the animals. The spurs help me to hang on. And my spurs are supposed to be in contact with the horse's shoulders each time the bronc's front hooves hit the ground."

She touched a rowel lightly and looked up at him as he reached into a hip pocket.

"Here's a program. When this is over, I'll take you to dinner." Stretching his arm across her, he took folders from Merry's bag. He leaned close, and she noticed the scent of him, felt his arm rest lightly on her knee. "Here are some things you can take home to look over," he said. "Here's my last physical, so you'll know I'm as healthy as that horse I'll ride," he said, thrusting papers into her hand. "Blood test, complete physical. Here's a list of my assets and net worth. At the moment I don't owe any money to anyone. Here are my brothers' addresses and phone numbers."

Astounded, Faith looked at the papers he'd placed in her hand. "You don't need to do this!"

"Sure, I do," he answered easily. "If we're marrying, you should know what you're getting into."

"We're not marrying," she said, wondering whether he was listening to her. His dark eyes drifted over her, and she became aware of herself, of her pale yellow silk blouse, her tan slacks. She could see the approval in his warm gaze, feel that swift arc of tension that erased the world and narrowed existence down to just the two of them.

He leaned closer to brush a light kiss on Faith's lips, just the faintest touch, yet it made her want to close her eyes, slip her arm around his neck and deepen the kiss.

"We'll discuss it later. But before I go, let me pin your earring to my hat for good luck," he said, taking one of the stud diamond earrings from her ear, his knuckles brushing her cheek and ear lightly. "Okay?" he asked, hesitating only inches from her.

"Okay," she barely answered, looking at his mouth and remembering his kisses.

He pulled off his hat, punched the earring through the band and fastened it next to the feathers.

"Why the feathers? More good luck?"

"Something like that. They came from Granddad's farm. That's why they're battered. I've had those feathers a long time." He glanced over his shoulder. "See that gate? I'll come out there and hopefully ride here in front of you. And let's hope Demon Rum doesn't toss me right into your lap."

Amusement danced in his dark eyes, but she couldn't share it. "I'm not certain I can stand to watch you. I've never fainted in my life, but if you get stomped on by a ten-ton bull—I'll pass out."

"Why, darlin', you *do* care!" he teased, stroking her cheek lightly. The contact was slight, yet it kindled a desire that was ready to blaze. "See you later," he added, grinning as he rose to leave.

He settled his hat on his head and went down the steps, vaulting the wall before dropping into the arena to head toward the gate. She watched his long-legged stride, appraised his broad shoulders and the black hair secured behind his head. Her pulse drummed in a steady beat of excitement. Why did everything seem more vivid, more intense, since she had met him?

She glanced around the arena, with its dirt-covered floor and metal chutes, and she knew that if she closed her eyes a year from now, she would remember this night in fine clarity, as if everything that concerned Jared was etched in her memory. Never before had it been that way with any man she had dated. Maybe that came from having known them for years. But she knew that wasn't so. Never, at any point in time, had it been reckless and dazzling with any of them. And it never would. The realization startled her. She looked at Merry, who smiled at her.

"You little doll. No wonder he spoke all that silly baby talk to you," she said, leaning over Merry. The baby cooed and laughed and kicked her feet, drooling while her blue eyes sparkled.

Faith wiped Merry's chin with a cloth bib that was tucked into the bag. "You are a sweetie, and I have to admit, your daddy's pretty nice, too. Maybe a little headstrong."

Faith glanced down at the papers in her lap and picked up his physical, glancing over statistics. The man had a clean bill of health. She felt a flicker of relief, because she suspected he was the kind of man who attracted women in droves, and she imagined until Merry came along, he'd had a relatively casual attitude toward sex.

His blood pressure was good, his cholesterol level fine. Heart and lungs fine. Then came a staggering roster of sprains, fractures and broken bones: broken thumb, broken fingers, fractured shoulder, sprained ankle, broken collarbone, broken arm, broken wrist, broken leg, broken ribs. The list was long, and she wondered if it was all from bronc and bull riding.

Shifting to the page of assets, she glanced over figures and was shocked. She knew her impression of him was prejudiced by his lollygagging in the park. He seemed like a drifter, and she hadn't thought of him as having so much as a bank account, but the figures on the page were impressive. She straightened the papers on her knees and really studied the figures.

He had sizable savings, plus his house on Peoria, which had been appraised and was worth about what Faith would have guessed for a house in that area of town. A trust from Dusty had been set up for Merry. Faith had suspected that one reason for Jared's proposal might have been her steady job and nice income, yet now she knew that wasn't the case.

He hadn't proposed because of her income—he had plenty of his own. Faith looked at the figures again, unable to grasp that a man who did not work regular hours could have such a net worth. How could he spend his days in the park and still save money? She pulled out the page with his brothers' addresses. A picture of three boys was tacked to the page. It was a battered picture, taken years earlier, and she held it closer.

Jared had written down their names and drawn arrows pointing to each one. Jared looked the youngest, standing between the other two. All three had the same black hair, the broad firm jaw and prominent cheekbones. Faith had to admit that she found Jared to be the most handsome of the three rugged brothers.

Beneath the picture Jared had boldly scrawled vital statistics.

Wyatt: thirty-three, father of Kelsey and twin baby girls, Robin and Rachel. Wife is Alexa.

Matt: thirty-four, single—confirmed old bachelor. Wheat farmer in western Oklahoma.

Mother: Costa Whitewolf, died of drug overdose in a Wakulla hospital.

Grandfather: Loughlan Whitewolf. Grandmother: Cornelia Whitewolf. Own farm in southwestern Oklahoma near Lawton.

Faith lowered the paper, put it in the folder and placed the document in Merry's bag. The baby began to fuss and Faith unbuckled her, then lifted her out of her carrier.

"I'll bet you're tired of sitting there. Let's stand and look for your daddy, who will be riding a wild old bull. I may have to hold your hand and hide my eyes. Actually, I'm not sure either one of us should watch."

Merry gurgled and Faith cuddled her as she moved around the box. The seats began to fill up with people, and when the rodeo commenced, Faith held Merry up so she could watch the horses parade past in a grand procession during the opening ceremonies.

The first event was bareback riding, and Merry began to fuss, so Faith placed her on a seat, changed her and then picked her up to give her a bottle.

As she fed the baby, she watched the first horse leap out

of the chute and buck, the rider flying off and landing hard. She shut her eyes the next time a ride began. Her palms were damp. How could Jared earn a living this way?

Calf roping followed, and she could bear to watch it. Then the clowns performed, and after their act, saddle bronc riding was scheduled. Faith's nervousness increased. She hadn't been able to watch men she didn't know get tossed around. How would she be able to watch one she did care about? And she did care. Though his arrival in her life had caused upheaval and stirred longings she should probably ignore, she had to admit, she liked being with him.

At the sound of the buzzer, the first rider burst out of the chute. Faith drew a deep breath, horrified as the horse bucked and spun and the man was thrown, hitting the ground hard, sending up puffs of dust. The man looked as if he would be stomped beneath the hooves, but he rolled and jumped to his feet, scooped up his hat and exited to applause while pickup cowboys got the horse out of the arena. Faith looked down at Merry, who was gazing back with solemn blue eyes.

"Your daddy is going to ride third, but I suppose you'll be more interested in staying where you are and drinking your bottle."

Merry continued to suck, and Faith looked up as the buzzer sounded again and another wild horse leaped out of the chute. This time the man rode longer, getting tossed just a second before the buzzer sounded. He landed on his back and jumped up as easily as the first cowboy had, and she wondered again about Jared. What kind of man was he to enjoy this sort of sport and earn his living at it?

In the chute she could see his black hat, see him looking down at his horse. The roan bucked, slamming hooves into the chute and banging around while the announcer continued speaking, stating Jared's name and winnings. Then the buzzer sounded and the gate swung open.

The roan shot into the air. Jared's feet swung forward, stroking back and forth while he held one hand high in the air. Watching as his hat flew off and he stayed in the saddle, she held her breath. The horse twisted and bucked, moving closer to her box. Faith could hear the hooves thud against the dirt, hear the animal's snorts until they were drowned out by applause and cheers. She squeezed her eyes closed, then opened an eye to watch.

The buzzer sounded and the applause was loud. Jared slid onto the back of a pickup rider's horse and then jumped down, leaving the roan to others as he strode to scoop up his hat, then thumped it against his leg, which was covered by his chaps. Turning her way, he waved and then headed for the fence, where he swung his long legs over and dropped down on the other side.

Her palms were damp, she had bitten her lip, and she gulped for air, trying to catch her breath after holding it during his ride. She didn't want to watch him ride a bull. A horse had been bad enough.

She looked down at Merry, whose eyes were closed as she busily sucked on the bottle.

"Your daddy is wild and tough and crazy and charming. As adorable as you are, I can't be part of his life. Not in the next million years," she whispered.

Five

Steer wrestling was the next event, and it seemed violent in its own way, though not as bad as the bronc riding. Next came team roping, followed by barrel racing, and for a moment Faith enjoyed the rodeo, watching the pretty women ride like the wind, the horses performing with grace and amazing speed.

The clowns gave an exhibition, and Faith was sorry Merry had fallen asleep, yet even the clowns' antics with the powerful bull gave her some tense moments.

The last event was bull riding. Jared was first and Faith didn't think she could watch. Merry slept peacefully in her arms, and Faith drew a deep breath, watching Jared prepare himself in the chute.

The buzzer sounded and the gate swung open.

The huge gray bull stormed out of the chute, flinging Jared around like a toy, yet he clung to the animal's back as it twisted and bucked and kicked. The animal looked like a monster with its wide horns and massive body. Faith felt faint and hot, terrified for Jared, knowing she would be equally petrified for every rider. Unable to watch, she closed her eyes. If Jared was hurt or stomped, she wouldn't be able to stand it.

The buzzer sounded. Applause and cheers and whistles filled the arena. She opened her eyes and saw the bull twist in the air. Jared flew off, landing on his side as the animal charged.

Faith cried out, clutching the rail with one hand, her other arm around Merry. Jared rolled out of the way and jumped up to run for the gate while the clowns waved hats at the bull, who charged after Jared for a few feet and then swerved to chase a clown.

Sinking back in the seat, Faith watched Jared climb over the fence and disappear from view. She wiped her damp palm on her slacks, tried to catch her breath and waited for her heart to stop pounding. The next rider came out of the chute, and not wanting to watch, she looked down at Merry. At a gasp from the crowd, Faith glanced up and saw the rider sprawled on the dirt. While men ran out to help him, the clowns distracted the bull, dodging when it charged them.

The next rider did better, but he didn't last until the buzzer sounded.

"How'd you like your first rodeo?" Jared asked as he dropped into a seat beside her.

"I was terrified. I don't know how you can do that!"

He grinned. Dirt was smudged on his face and he had a scrape on his cheek. "I may win a lot of money."

"Did you ever think of taking up accounting or something sane and sensible?"

He laughed and touched her nose. Pulling off his hat, he unfastened her earring. "This brought me great luck," he said, "just like I thought it would."

"I think you've had a lot of luck before without my earring," she answered dryly, her heart fluttering because he was so close.

Leaning forward, he replaced the diamond stud in her ear, his fingers brushing her ear and throat while his face hovered only inches from hers. He smelled faintly of dust and leather and sweat. She looked at his mouth, the slightly full lower lip, and she remembered how it had felt to have his mouth on hers. His dark gaze met hers and her pulse jumped.

"Let's go," he said. "I'll put Merry in her carrier."

He took the baby gently from Faith's arms, his hands brushing over Faith, and then he knelt down to buckle Merry in her baby seat. He picked up the carrier and bag and took Faith's arm to head for the door. As they climbed steps, she heard the announcer's loud voice state that Jared Whitewolf had won bull riding.

"You don't have to stick around?"

"Not tonight. I'm accumulating points. I'll be back tomorrow night. We're going now."

We. Excitement bubbled within Faith, but she sternly reminded herself she was going to say no to Jared's proposal. She had rehearsed it dozens of times, imagining his arguments, her firm refusal and their goodbye.

This time Jared drove to a crowded restaurant on the city's edge, where they sat in a corner booth. The tables were wooden, the floor terrazzo, and tantalizing smells of roasting meat and a wood-burning fire filled the room. Merry continued to sleep, her hands folded peacefully in her lap.

"She's an angel, Jared."

"That she is."

They ordered, and over juicy ribs covered in thick red barbecue sauce, Jared asked her once again about her work.

"So you could open your own office if you wanted to and do the same thing you're doing now?"

"Yes, I could. And maybe someday I will. At the moment, I'm happy where I am and don't want the responsibility of starting up my own company."

"Seems like you already know a lot of people who

would want you to continue to handle their accounts. You could work from a ranch just as well as from a downtown office.''

She met his satisfied gaze and felt both annoyed and amused. "You think you'll figure everything out all by yourself?''

He shrugged. "I'm looking at possibilities.''

"Well, then, look at the possibility of getting yourself a regular nine-to-five job, hiring a nanny, dating someone for months and then proposing.''

"That isn't what I want to do. Nor is it necessary. I'll be able to take care of Merry by riding in rodeos and ranching. You saw what I earn.''

"Yes, I did.''

"Surprised you, didn't I?'' he asked, and this time there was no mistaking the amusement that danced in his dark eyes. "You have me pegged as a vagabond adventurer.''

"Income or no income, you're still a drifter in my eyes.''

"I'll work on my image,'' he said, and she wondered if she had handed him a challenge.

While they finished their ribs, the crowd thinned. Conversation turned to their families once again.

"Have your grandparents seen Merry?'' she asked.

"Yes, I stayed with them right after Dusty died. They had five other children besides Mom and three of the children live on farms in the area, so Grandmom has a lot of children and grandchildren underfoot. The rest of the family is pretty settled. Much more like your family. My brothers and I were the wild bunch.'' He leaned forward to trail his fingers lightly over her wrist and hand.

"I'm going to prove to you that I can settle down like a rock in the bottom of a pond. When Dusty died and I was given Merry, some of the married guys' wives helped me look after her for a few days while we buried Dusty. He didn't have any other family, so I planned the funeral and took care of the legal stuff. Then I packed up and took Merry home to Grandmom. She showed me how to take care of the baby. I had a rodeo already scheduled in Arizona, in the Turquoise Prorodeo Circuit, so Merry and I went west and now we're headed back. I want to see my brothers this time. I figured Grandmom had told them about Merry by now, but she must not have told Wyatt."

"So there is some stability in your life."

His dark eyes filled with amusement. "Does that make your heart flutter with relief? Or give me just a tad more chance with you? Granddad and my grandmother are as stable as your family. They've been on their farm since it was handed to them by the U.S. Government when they doled out land to the Indians." He reached out to slip his hand behind her neck. "And when I settle, I intend to settle for good."

"You yourself said you can't plan out everything," she said, feeling consumed by his dark eyes, aware of his fingers lightly trailing back and forth across her nape. He was as dangerous to her world as a stalking tiger. What recklessness in her drew her to danger? She knew she should have said goodbye. Yet here she was, biding her time with a daredevil who mesmerized her.

"I plan to settle," he replied. "I'll do the rodeo circuit, but I'm coming home to the same house and my family."

"Jared, that sounds lovely, but you and me—well, it's absolutely impossible."

"Let's go where we can talk with a little more privacy." He picked up Merry and slid out of the booth.

When they stepped outside, it was as nice a night as the previous one, with a bright full moon and a cool spring breeze. Jared draped his arm across her shoulders and walked silently beside her.

Once they'd settled themselves in the pickup, they drove through the city, and at the top of a hill they marveled at the view of the lights of downtown Tulsa. To the west was the dark ribbon of the Arkansas River; to the east, lights shone brightly in residential areas.

When they reached Faith's condo, Jared drove through

the iron gates and parked in her driveway. He picked up the sleeping baby in her carrier.

As soon as they were inside Faith's home, Merry woke suddenly, and by the time Jared unbuckled her from the baby carrier, she was crying loudly.

"I'll take her," Faith said, reaching for her, "while you get her bottle ready."

Faith was aware of her hands brushing his arms and chest as she took Merry from him. "Come here," she said to Merry, heading toward her bedroom, "and let's change you and put on your pj's and get you ready for sleepy land."

Merry bawled and kicked, clearly not interested in Faith's chatter.

Jared appeared at the door, bottle in hand. "Let me have my girl, and we'll stop all that ruckus." His gaze went over the room and Faith blushed, imagining how sterile and pristine it would look to him.

He crossed the room, and his utter masculinity seemed to invade the area. She knew she would remember him being in her bedroom forever.

"This is where you sleep." He looked into her eyes, and the fiery heat she saw in his made her insides quiver and her breath catch. And she wondered what had been dancing in his imagination. Whatever it had been, she was sure it involved her.

He took Merry from her, and little hands grabbed the bottle Jared held as Merry jammed it into her mouth.

"Miss Piggy," he remarked with amusement. "You'd think she hadn't eaten for days instead of hours." He turned and sat on the white rocker. "Is this okay?"

"Sure," Faith answered, sitting on the foot of the bed, kicking off her low-heeled shoes, amazed how he seemed perfectly at home in her bedroom. He looked completely relaxed while she felt edgy, too aware of him in these intimate surroundings that she had considered a very private part of her life. He had pulled free the snaps on the upper part of his shirt, leaving part of his chest bare. He dominated the room, looking as incongruous in her white-and-blue frilly bedroom as a tiger in a bubble bath.

"Have you ever ridden a horse, Faith?"

"Yes, I've ridden, but not in years. I had lessons and rode pretty regularly when I was about ten, but that's the last. Have you ever been to the symphony?"

He shook his head. "No, but I'm willing to try it."

She could imagine his taste in music, suspecting their tastes in everything from entertainment to vacations were vastly different. "Where are the family pictures?" he asked, glancing around the room.

"In the spare bedroom. There's a wall of them."

"When Merry finishes, you can show me."

"There are so many of us, it's confusing."

"We have lots of aunts and uncles and cousins, so I'm accustomed to the jumble of a big family."

"If you left home at sixteen, you can't really be accustomed to a family at all."

"Not so. By age sixteen you've been through the formative years. And I've gone back to the farm off and on."

"I couldn't help but notice your medical history in the files you gave me. Was it from riding in rodeos that you had all those broken bones?"

"Yeah. That and one broken arm from the sorry bastard who was my mother's common-law husband number four."

"How awful!"

"He didn't last long in our lives, thank the Lord. Our mother could really pick 'em. They were as wild as she was." Jared continued to rock, and he looked down at Merry as she played with his chin. He turned and playfully bit her fingers and growled. She laughed, little bubbles of milk curling out of the corners of her mouth. Then she returned to drinking her milk and running her fingers along his jaw.

"Did you like the rodeo?" he asked Merry. "Did you

watch your daddy ride the big bull? Someday you'll ride your own horse.''

Faith watched as Jared spoke softly to Merry while he fed her. His long legs were stretched out in front of him, his boots were dusty, and she remembered the feel of his long, lean body pressed against hers. Her gaze trailed back up, over his jeans, Merry in his arms, his broad shoulders— to meet his gaze.

Embarrassed to be caught so openly looking him over, she blushed.

Merry finished her bottle, and Jared lifted her to his shoulder, patting her back. ''Let's go meet the family,'' he said to Faith, standing.

Faith switched on the light in another bedroom that held a queen-size bed and had a maroon and deep hunter green decor. All the time she explained who each person was in the family pictures, she was acutely aware of Jared brushing against her, shoulder to shoulder, his hand lightly resting on her shoulder, then moving to her nape.

By the time they finished, Merry was asleep again and Faith was tied in knots from all his light touches. ''I'll get a blanket,'' she said. ''Can I put her on the bed? She won't roll off if I put pillows around her.''

They laid Merry down and then switched off the light before venturing for the kitchen. But as they crossed through the living room, Jared took Faith's arm and turned her to face him. ''I've been waiting since last night to be alone with you,'' he said quietly, drawing her to him.

Her pulse jumped and her heart thudded. Now was the time to say no, but any resistance vanished as she met his smoldering gaze. She wanted to be in his arms, wanted his kisses. It didn't mean she wanted to marry him, she told herself fleetingly, the thought swept away the moment his arm tightened around her waist and he bent his head.

His mouth covered hers, and she trembled. Desire, hot as a flame, burned in her, making an ache low in her body, a basic need that was as strong as the need to breathe.

Again, she caught the scent of his aftershave and a faint masculine smell of sweat and leather. Her senses reeled. His kisses were powerful, heady stuff.

He fitted her to his body, one hand holding her tightly while the other ran through her hair. She felt his arousal, knew he wanted her. And she was discovering she had never wanted a man before as much as she wanted this one. Touching each other was a marvel, each kiss intoxicating. She loved the excitement, the challenge of him. He was the wrong person for her, she knew, but his kisses felt so right.

His shoulders were hard beneath her hands. She slipped her fingers across the strong column of his neck. The leather thong that tied his hair came loose, and coarse, long strands fell over her wrists, reminding her what an unknown element he was, a man who was as headstrong as he was fearless.

His hand inched slowly along her throat, sliding lower, a prolonged torment until his hand reached her breast, stroking so lightly, making her gasp and moan. Her breasts tightened. The ache she felt increased, and she yearned for more. His hand slipped beneath the silk blouse, cupping her breast.

He pushed away the filmy lace bra and caressed her nipple, his thumb drawing circles that tantalized. She caught his hand, trying to inject sanity into the moment, feeling caught on a thundering roller coaster of passion that could wreck her quiet life.

"Jared, wait," she gasped, torn between wanting him desperately and knowing she had to stop.

He stopped the sensuous onslaught to look at her while she struggled for breath and pulled her clothes in place. They both were breathing hard. She had felt his heartbeat and knew it was as erratic as her own. This tall cowboy was riding roughshod over her defenses, smashing them with kisses that melted resistance and good sense. But his racing heart told her that he felt something, too.

He fumbled in his pocket and pulled out a small box. "Marry me, Faith," he said, opening the box.

A ring glittered in the dim light from the hall. The sparkling light from the purity of the stone dazzled, dancing before her eyes, a surprise and a temptation. The diamond's brilliance held promises of excitement, of life as she had never dared to experience it. And craziness.

How could she even consider marriage?

She stared at the ring while Jared removed it from the box. Then he took her hand, pausing to look at her quizzically.

"I can't," she whispered. Struggling to find her voice and speak firmly, her gaze stayed on the ring. "I've told you all the reasons," she said, mechanically following her lifelong habits, customary caution and sensible plans.

"My reasons why we should marry are better. You know we have something between us you've never known before," he said. "And neither have I. This is special for me, too, Faith." He tilted her face to look at him, and she could feel the force of his determination wrap around her heart.

"I want you. We can fall in love later."

"Let's fall in love first."

"I need you now. Merry needs a mother."

"Get a nanny!" she snapped, coming out of her daze.

"I want you for my wife. There doesn't have to be a physical union until you're ready."

"That's the least of the problems!" she said, knowing it took all her will to keep from pulling him toward the bedroom. "I don't know you! We're not in love!"

"Take a chance, Faith." His voice was deep and strong and maddeningly sure. "You know you're not happy with your life right now. You love little babies and you want one. I'm offering you what you want."

"I'm not ready for this," she whispered, feeling panicked.

But she was drawn to the wildness in him, that streak that let him do what he wanted. He lived a life she had never dared. She had always done what was expected, followed in the footsteps of the rest of her family. They lived in the same part of town, they went to the same church. She worked for her uncle. She dated men like her brothers and father. She lived an orderly, routine life that was completely predictable and secure.

But here was a whirlwind who promised no such stability. He was a great unknown, an adventurer, wild and dangerous. He was a wanderer who followed his whims. Staring at him, she was silent while her emotions warred like fierce combatants.

"If you say no, I'm gone," he informed her quietly. "I'm not hanging around like those guys you've known all your life. I'm not into long courtships."

"How do I know you're into marriage?"

His dark eyes blasted her with a fire that burned to her heart. "I know what I want," he said in a husky, forceful voice. "I always have. Marry me."

If she said no, she knew he would disappear out of her life forever. She had no doubts about it. She was certain this man didn't bluff or speak idly. And if he did leave tonight, would she forever feel she had thrown away a lifetime of happiness?

"I have to have a church wedding," she said, barely giving it a thought, merely stalling while her mind raced.

"Fine. Just don't drag it out. Merry needs a mother."

She should tell him goodbye. Let him go. He was proposing to her in order to gain a nanny. That was the basic reason, but she knew better than that. There was something spectacular between them. He felt it, too.

"Faith, you know what your heart is telling you. This is right. I can feel it to my soul."

"I can't do it. I just can't do it. It's so against everything in my life," she said, wanting to wring her hands and grind her teeth. "It's against my family, my upbringing, my good judgment. No, I can't."

He placed the ring in the box and closed it, then put it

in his pocket. He brushed a kiss on her lips and passed her as he went to the bedroom to get Merry.

This tall, exciting cowboy was going to walk out of her life forever, and she would go back to empty nights and empty weekends and long hours of work and nothing else.

He came back with Merry, who was still asleep. Faith followed him to the kitchen. He placed his hat on his head and paused with his hand on the doorknob while he gave Faith a long, enigmatic look. "I'll miss you," he said softly. He opened the door, stepped outside and was gone.

Six

She looked around the empty kitchen. Was this what she wanted? She thought about standing in Jared's arms. She remembered holding Merry.

He was walking out of her life forever. She had no idea how to find him.

Did she want to live her life the way she always had? Did she want the same routine all the rest of her life? The same job?

Did she want a baby?

Everything inside her screamed to go after him. *Take a risk for once!*

He adored Merry and took good care of her. He was solvent, had plans for his future. His kisses were magic, the chemistry between them impossible to ignore. What was she waiting for—a clone of her brothers and her father? And here was her chance for a baby.

She couldn't let him go. With a pounding heart, she dashed across the kitchen and out the back door. He was leaning over the back seat of the pickup, buckling Merry's carrier in.

"Jared!"

He straightened and turned to face her. She stopped only a few feet from him. The wind caught locks of her hair and blew them across her cheek. She brushed them away.

"Yes, I'll marry you," she said in a rush, her heart beating so loudly that her own voice sounded strange and dim. He didn't move, and she wondered whether he had changed his mind.

"Do you know what you're doing?" he asked.

She shook her head. "No. I just don't want you to go."

He closed the space between them and pulled her to him tightly while he leaned down to kiss her hard, a breathtaking kiss that made her forget the proposal, her acceptance, everything except him. His tongue stroked hers, went deep into her mouth and she trembled, clinging to him, returning his kiss. She felt as if she had let go of that cliff she had been slipping over and now was tumbling into a raging river.

She slid her hands across his broad shoulders, wound her arms around his neck, relishing the solid strength of him and praying that he would be as good a husband as he was a father. As she melted against him, she knew her life would never be the same as it had been before she charged through the spirea bushes. This tall cowboy was taking her with him on his wild ride through life. Shock, uncertainty, doubts—all burned to vapor and vanished. Bubbling excitement pumped through her veins, and she returned his kiss. Their tongues tangled, slick, hot, an intimate promise and bond. Her heart pounded violently. The cowboy and the baby—her husband, her child. This cowboy's seductive proposal was impossible to resist.

He raised his head and she felt a loss. She opened her eyes to find him watching her in that disturbing manner he had. Moonlight spilled over her face, but he was in shadow. He reached into his pocket and pulled out the small box, withdrawing the ring again. He put away the box and held her hand, pausing before he said, "Will you marry me, Faith?"

"Yes," she answered.

He slipped the ring on her finger, then pulled her to him to kiss her again, brushing her lips with his. His mouth was firm and warm, the slight stubble on his jaw tickling her tender skin.

"You won't regret it," he said softly. "I promise to do everything in my power to make you happy. We'll make a good family." His mouth covered hers again, another fiery kiss that shook her. His kisses trailed to her ear. "I could grow to love you, darlin'," he whispered.

He bent his head, his mouth taking and giving, tongues tangling and desire escalating. With each kiss she felt needed. Each one carried her to a more dizzying height than the ones before and made her want so much more. At the same time, she felt uncertain and knew they had to have some clear understandings. She pushed lightly against his chest and he raised his head.

"Jared, we should talk about this." He ran his hand along her throat and she inhaled, feeling as if she was gasping to breathe. "I know we're attracted to each other, but you said it could be a marriage of convenience. I like your kisses," she admitted, blushing hotly, "but you have to give me some time. You don't want to wait to marry. I want to wait for the physical part so we can get to know each other. So there's a chance we'll really fall in love and not mistake lust for the real thing."

"Whatever you want," he said quietly. "We'll wait as long as you want to."

She drew a deep breath, wondering what kind of bargain she was making. This was not the marriage she had always imagined. "You still want to marry right away under those conditions?"

"I told you, I know what I want." He brushed a light kiss across her lips, lingering, making her want to step back into his arms. "Besides, darlin'," he whispered, stroking her ear with his tongue and sending little streaks of fire through her, "I don't think this waiting is going to be as long as you imagine."

She couldn't resist and turned her mouth to his for another long kiss. When he released her, she gazed up at him.

"Want to come back inside?" she asked.

He shook his head. "I'll put Merry to bed. Give you time to think about your wedding plans. Let's marry soon, Faith. Here's my hotel phone number," he said, pulling out a slip of paper.

"*Hotel?* I thought you said you own a home on Peoria." She stared at him while doubts hit her like a wave of ice water.

"I do. Dusty left the house to me, and we can go look at it tomorrow and see what you want to do to it. Right now, Merry and I are staying at a hotel."

She closed her eyes. "What else don't I know? How many other surprises are there?"

He caught her chin, brushed a kiss across her lips. "You'll adapt real well, darlin'. You efficient types always do. You'll move in and straighten up my life and get everything to suit yourself. We'll go to the rodeo tomorrow night, and sometime soon, I better meet your folks."

"I'll make arrangements. They're going to faint, Jared. Right in front of your eyes. Worse, my brothers may punch you out."

His white teeth flashed in a grin. "I'd bet my pickup that your brothers aren't the punching type. I'm not worried."

"You're right, I think. They can get a little worked up sometimes. And my grandfather—oh, my! Grandpa Kolanko says exactly what he thinks."

"I'll go with you to break the news, especially to Grandpa. I'll call you when I get to the hotel."

"What have I done?"

He pulled her to him again for one more devastating kiss

that left her wanting more. His mouth was fire and heady wine, every kiss bubbling worries away.

"See, you're ready for marriage," he said in a husky voice while his hand slid from her shoulder blade, down her spine, slowly and surely moving to her hip.

"Don't rush me."

"I wouldn't think of it," he drawled, and went around the pickup to climb behind the wheel. He waved, and she watched him drive away before she went inside and locked the door. Holding up her hand, she looked at her ring. It sparkled in the light and was big enough to impress her family.

At the thought of her family, her stomach knotted. Had she lost her mind? Jared Whitewolf had come into her life like a whirlwind. She touched the ring. She was going to be a wife and a mother. Something warm and joyous blossomed inside her and melted her fears.

In a daze, she moved through her condo and headed for her bedroom. Pulling on a blue cotton nightie, she got ready for bed and went over the events of the night. Long after dark she lay in bed, staring into the darkness, remembering their conversation. And she knew one thing—she wanted a baby of her own.

If this crazy marriage worked, it would be wonderful. If it didn't, this was her chance to have her own precious baby. Merry would be his. But *their* baby would be hers. At the thought of having her own baby, of being a mother to Merry and another baby, Faith let out her breath while joy filled her.

Scrambling out of bed, she switched on a light, got a pen and paper and began making a list, studying it thoughtfully. Then she retrieved the paper with Jared's phone number. She punched numbers, waited and asked for his room number.

"Hello." His deep greeting came out in a slow drawl.

"Were you asleep?"

"No, darlin'," he answered easily. "Just lying here thinking about you."

His words and sexy tone feathered a fuzzy warmth inside her. "Jared, I've been thinking about our—" She paused. It was difficult to get out the words. It still was dreamlike, impossible. She was marrying this cowboy she barely knew. "Our marriage," she said firmly, trying to view it as she would an ad campaign. "I think I should make clear what I want. *You* want a mother for Merry, and I'm happy with that. But I want—"

Again, words failed her. She was thankful she didn't have to look into his probing brown eyes. She was across town from him, yet she couldn't get out the words. She felt hot with embarrassment and then annoyed with herself for acting so foolish. "I want a baby," she blurted.

"I know that," he answered softly. "And we'll do our best. Whenever you're ready."

She wiped her damp palms and sighed. "Also," she said, running her finger down her list, "you'll agree to live in town for a couple of years before we try ranching?"

"We'll move when the time is right," he answered, and his amusement was clear. "Checking your list?"

She felt another wave of embarrassment. "As a matter of fact, yes. I'll call Mom, and we'll make arrangements to get together with my parents this weekend."

"Fine. I'm riding in a rodeo in Oklahoma City next weekend. I promised my brothers I would see them, and then I'm going to visit my grandparents. So get out your calendar, Faith, and let's pick the wedding date."

She picked up her calendar and looked into the next month. "How about the thirtieth of May?"

"How about the twenty-seventh of April or the second of May?"

"I can't possibly!"

"Sure, you can. Let's not postpone it. That was part of the deal. I have a rodeo the first weekend in May. We can marry and go to Colorado Springs for the rodeo."

"I'll call tomorrow to see about the church and let you know. Jared, you'll still have to get a nanny so I can continue working."

"Maybe. With my rodeo schedule, you and Merry will be with me weekends and you'll watch her while I ride. During the week, I can be home with her or take her with me to look at land. I have to buy land before I can start working as a rancher."

He waited, listening to silence, wondering if she was crossing nanny off her list.

"I don't know if it'll work out that way."

"If it doesn't, we'll make the right adjustments. If you get pregnant, are you going to keep right on working? You know you could work from home."

"I don't know. Jared, a lot of my friends who've married don't get pregnant real easily."

"I can't think of anything more pleasant to try to accomplish," he drawled, and listened to another silence. "Are you there, Faith?"

"Yes. And I guess that covers everything for now. You have this worked out in your head as much as I do in my list."

"Mine's a little looser. I adapt real easily."

"I hope you can adapt real easily to my family."

"Tell me all the family names and kids' ages again."

She set aside the tablet, calendar and pen and settled against the pillows to talk to him. After a time, she switched off the light and slid down in bed, listening to the rumble of his voice while he told her about his granddad's farm and the horse he liked best. And she realized when he talked about his grandparents, his tone of voice softened. That part of his childhood, at least, held good memories, and she was reassured to know there was a degree of security in his past.

Talk went from family to movies to sports. He explained bronc riding and bull riding to her, telling her how each event was scored, talking about the animals on the rodeo circuit.

She grew sleepy, wondering how much her life would change.

"Darlin'?"

"Hmm?"

"Are you falling asleep?"

"I suppose."

"I wish you were in my arms. Do you remember our kisses?"

"Too well," she answered, feeling her body tighten and desire flare.

"Good. You keep remembering, because I sure do. What we have is good, darlin'. It's very special. 'Night, Faith."

"Good night," she whispered softly, and switched off the phone. She glanced at the clock and received a stab of surprise. Almost half past four in the morning. How could she have talked so late? She rubbed her head on the pillow and closed her eyes, dreaming of being in his arms.

Jared lay in the darkness with his hands behind his head, thinking about his conversation with Faith. The woman was efficient, a planner. She wanted a baby—that had been plain the first few minutes he'd known her. She was restless, no longer satisfied with only a career. With his proposal, she now saw a chance to get the baby she had been dreaming about.

He could imagine Faith sitting in bed with her list in front of her, planning out her future. *Get pregnant, have baby, go back to regular life and wonderful career—and tell the cowboy goodbye.* She would have baby and career, and her life would be complete. Had he rushed her too much? Should he have opted for courting and winning her love first instead of pushing for marriage?

He rubbed his jaw. No reason the courting and winning couldn't come after the ceremony. Faith had asked for time before they consummated the marriage. Well, he would give the lady time. He had never planned much beyond the next rodeo, but he was going to plan now. After their wedding ceremony, he would try to win his lady's love.

Restless, he shoved aside the sheet and crossed the room to the window, looking down at the street below. A car moved along the empty street, lights throwing yellow circles on the dark pavement. He could see downtown Tulsa, but he wasn't facing the south part of the city where Faith lived. He could imagine her soundly asleep, satisfied with her plans.

He rubbed his jaw with the back of his hand. Could he make her happy? He was only a cowboy, pure country, and she was used to city suits. *I'm not good enough for the lady,* he thought, knowing that was exactly how her family would feel.

And what did he know about a happy marriage? Almost nothing—only what he had experienced at his grandparents' farm. He hadn't grown up with loving parents. Far from it. Three people's happiness was at stake here—had he moved too fast?

He recalled holding Faith in his arms, but doubts mingled with memories. There was a lot more to love and marriage than fiery kisses and rapturous loving.

He moved to Merry's small portable bed and brushed his knuckles over her soft cheek. A year ago, he would have packed and run from the prospect of marriage, but now, although scary, it seemed right.

Unsettled and unable to shake his doubts, he moved back to the window. He stood with his hands on his bare hips, his thoughts on the future while he gazed out over the city. He wanted a ranch and he thought he could manage one. He had good savings, and his granddad said he would help him get started.

Mulling over his future, Jared stared into the darkness. Could he pry Faith loose from her cushy job? She could do the same job from a ranch, and for a time she could drive back and forth into town if he could find land not too far out of the city. That didn't worry him. What was important was winning his lady's love.

On Sunday, the sense of being wrapped in a dream deepened. Faith spent the afternoon looking at the house on Peoria, a two-story frame with oak floors and a large porch with Doric columns. It was hers to decorate, and she made lists and measured and was aware of Jared's dark eyes constantly on her. He didn't care what she did with the place, and during the afternoon as he stood in the backyard, looking up at one of the large oaks, she wondered about him. He was so easygoing, with no particular roots except for his grandparents. He had been deeply hurt by the loss of his friend, but other than that, he seemed to take life as it came. Would he ever fall deeply in love? Would she? Her gaze ran across his broad shoulders and down to trim hips, and she remembered their first meeting and the sight of his bare, muscled chest. She was going to be his wife in less than a month.

By four o'clock, the dream was beginning to transform into a nightmare. Her nerves felt raw, her stomach knotted, and she rehearsed a dozen scenarios of how to break the news of her engagement to her parents.

She had called her mother, told her she had someone important she wanted them to meet and that she had some big news.

Jared had taken her home to change, and he came back to pick her up at six o'clock. One of Jared's friends, Will MacGiver, was keeping Merry at his farm near Tulsa. Jared had taken Merry to Will's before picking up Faith.

Through the window, she watched Jared climb out of his pickup. Looking every inch a cowboy, he wore a turquoise-and-black Western shirt, one of his fancy belt buckles, his jeans, boots and hat. Her parents would go into shock.

Nervous and unable to feel comfortable in anything, Faith had dressed four times, finally deciding on red slacks and a red blouse.

As they drove along the winding drive beneath stately oaks to her parents' two-story Tudor house, she wanted to flee. Her panic deepened when she saw a black car and a green utility vehicle parked in front of the garage.

"Oh, my word. My sisters are here! Did I tell you that all of us live within a two-mile radius of my parents?"

"Whoops. I'm afraid I can't promise that."

"We don't have to live that close. Jared, I should have told my folks first and then brought you to meet them."

"This will be all right," he said.

"How can you be so calm?" she snapped, wondering if anything ruffled his feathers.

He wound his fingers through hers, picked up her hand to brush a kiss across her knuckles and looked at her with dark eyes that momentarily banished her fears.

The minute she stepped out of the pickup, her worries returned. Faith took a deep breath as Jared retrieved a folder from the back seat and turned to drape his arm across her shoulders.

"What's that?"

"I think your father is entitled to the same information about me that I gave you."

"You don't have to do that!" she said between clenched teeth. "Jared, we can't go through with this."

"We surely can. Want me to kiss you right here and now and help you remember part of why this is so right?"

"No! Mercy, mercy, no! Don't you dare kiss me while we're here."

"Your family doesn't approve of affection?"

"Stop teasing me! How can you be calm? We'll go in through the kitchen."

"Tell me their names once more."

"Andy is the oldest, and I'm the next oldest. Meg, who's married to Stan, follows, and then Keith and Alice. Andy has two boys—Brian is eight and Joshua is seven. Meg's Caleb is seven, Geoff is six, Nina is five and Mattie is four. Keith's Ben is three, and Alyssa is two. Alice's boys are

Derek, five, and Graham, three. Mom and Dad are Tom and Evelyn.''

"I doubt if your folks and I will be on a first-name basis for a time," Jared drawled.

"You don't have even one little butterfly in your stomach, do you?" she asked, getting annoyed by his calm.

"No, darlin', I really don't. Want to feel my stomach and see?" he asked, lowering her hand.

"No!" She yanked her hand away and heard his chuckle.

"They're part of you, so they have to be good," Jared added cheerfully.

She paused with her hand on the back doorknob. "Jared, how can you be so sure about me?"

He gazed at her solemnly, his dark eyes making her heart skip a beat, her family worries forgotten. "I know what I want. And I know what happens when we kiss. I'll never get enough of that."

His certainty bolstered her, and she took a deep breath before opening the door. They entered a hallway that opened to various rooms, including a large kitchen with a terrazzo floor and skylights that spilled light over the appliances and ash cabinets.

"Mom, Dad!"

A slender, attractive blonde appeared, smiling at Faith, curiosity in her eyes when she looked at Jared. A tall man with sandy hair, slightly graying at the temples, entered the room.

"Mom, Dad, this is Jared Whitewolf. Jared, meet my parents, Evelyn and Tom Kolanko."

"Glad to meet you," Jared said easily to her mom while he shook hands with her dad.

"Come in," her mom said. "Meg and Alice are here. I think Andy will be here in a few minutes."

The back door opened and two little boys spilled inside. They took one look at Jared and screeched to a halt to study him. A couple followed the children inside. Dressed in slacks and a golf shirt, Andy Kolanko stared at Faith with curious green eyes.

"Jared, this is my brother Andy, my sister-in-law Glenna, and my nephews Brian and Joshua."

Jared shook hands with Andy, who studied him with a cold stare.

"Are you a real cowboy?" Joshua asked in a child's high voice.

"Yes, I am."

"Are you an Indian?"

"Joshua!"

"It's all right. Yes, I'm Native American and I ride horses. Do you like to ride horses?"

Joshua nodded solemnly.

"Let's go in the other room," Faith's father said. "Otherwise, Joshua will ask you questions until sunup tomorrow."

The boys trailed after Jared, and Faith knew they were enthralled by his boots, belt buckle and hat. He removed his hat and placed it on a kitchen chair. Joshua reached for it and Andy picked it up out of his reach.

"That's all right," Jared remarked easily. "He can't hurt my hat. Let him wear it if he wants to."

Andy placed it high on a shelf, shaking his head at Joshua.

"Jared was in the rodeo last night and Friday night. He won bull riding and was second place in saddle bronc riding," Faith said, aware she was babbling, wiping her damp palms together as the group moved to the living room.

In the large family room, her sisters were picking up a puzzle spread on a game table. "Jared, I'd like you to meet my sisters, Meg and Alice. This is Jared Whitewolf."

Short, dimpled and brunette, Meg smiled broadly. Almost as tall as Faith and with sandy hair, Alice offered her hand. As everyone sat down, Jared glanced at her father. "If you folks will excuse us, I think it would be a good idea if I talked to you right away, Mr. Kolanko."

A startled look passed over her sisters' faces. Andy frowned. Faith saw her mother's chin drop, and her father nodded without batting an eye.

"We'll go to the guest room." He motioned to Jared, and the two men left the room with Faith's two little towheaded nephews trailing behind Jared. All the adults turned to stare at Faith.

She felt as if she were plunging into an icy pond. She took a deep breath and braced for the storm. "I'm engaged," she said, holding out her hand to show them her ring.

Her mother shrieked and fell back against the chair while Meg's mouth dropped open and Alice jumped up to run to their mother.

"You're what?" Andy asked.

"Engaged."

"To Hopalong Cassidy? When did you meet him? What in the hell do you two have in common? What about Earl?"

"I haven't dated Earl in five months and never will again," she said, answering the last question. "Mom, are you all right?"

"Who is this man?" her mother asked.

"He's a cowboy and I'm going to marry him."

"Oh, my word! Saints help us. Have you lost your senses?"

"Is this really my sister Faith?" Meg asked, staring at her. "Practical, her-future-mapped-out Faith?" Meg crossed the room to take Faith's hand and look at her ring. "My, that's nice. I'm impressed!"

"I'm not. How long have you known him?" Andy asked sharply.

"Long enough," Faith answered, suddenly feeling more sure in her decision.

"Does he have a farm?"

"No, he doesn't. But he has a bank account. That's what he's talking to Dad about."

"Well, damnation, you've lost your mind," Andy said.

"Andy! It's Faith's decision," Glenna said. "Stop being such a big brother."

The back door slammed shut, and Faith looked over her shoulder to see her younger brother Keith enter the room. Stocky, brunette like Meg, his green eyes held curiosity. "What's happening?"

"Faith's getting married!" Meg exclaimed. "To a cowboy."

Questions and protests swirled around Faith while she wondered what Jared and her father were doing. How would her father handle Jared?

"Does he have a ranch around here?" Andy persisted, and she knew her brother wouldn't stop until he found out all he could about Jared.

"He's a bull rider and a bronc rider. He owns a house on Peoria and he wants to buy a ranch."

"He's a bum," Andy snapped. "Hell's bells!"

"No, he's not!"

"The man doesn't have a job?" her mother asked, looking aghast.

"Where did you meet him?" Meg wanted to know.

"He was with his little girl at the park."

"My word, he's divorced and has children."

"One little baby and he's not divorced. He's never been married."

"Oh, my word. He has a baby and didn't marry the mother—"

"Mom, let me tell you about him," Faith said quietly, while Andy swore and moved restlessly around the room. Faith told them about Merry and how Jared came to adopt her while her brothers glared and her mother wrung her hands.

"Faith, make it a long engagement so you'll be sure," her mother urged quietly.

"Mom, we're getting married as soon as I can arrange it with the church."

"You can't do that!" Andy snapped.

"Andy, I'm grown. I'll be thirty soon."

"He isn't like us. Is his horse tied outside? Are you going to milk cows every morning?"

"If I need to," she answered quietly, looking at her tall, blond brother whose green eyes sparked with anger. They had always been close, and she knew his intentions were good even if he was annoying her.

"Andy, cool it," Meg said.

More questions came from all of them, and Faith answered them while everyone quieted. Her mother left to phone her sister. Meg and Alice had to step outside to see about the children.

"Let's go where we can talk undisturbed," Andy said, motioning to her and to Keith. Faith went to a back bedroom with them and Andy closed the door, turning to face her. "Have you lost your mind?"

"No. I know what I'm doing. Jared's nice."

"Nice isn't what's important. You can't possibly begin to know him. And he doesn't have a job."

"Let me run a credit check on him," Keith said. "I'll see what—"

"Stop that. He's showing Dad his credit background and his physical."

"Who are his parents and where do they live?"

Someone rapped lightly on the door. It opened and Jared stepped inside. "I've talked to your dad," he said easily, crossing the room to her. "Why don't you join your mother and sisters. We'll be along in a minute," he said. She looked at her brothers, who were glaring at Jared, and she wasn't certain that they would resist punching him. Particularly Andy.

She saw all three men were waiting for her to leave, so she closed the door behind her. Their voices were low, indistinguishable, as she stood listening a moment before she moved away.

When Jared returned, her brothers were tight-lipped and

quiet. Faith heard the back door open and braced for the next onslaught. It could be only one person.

Grandpa Morgan Kolanko strode into the room. Stocky, with white strands running through his sandy hair, he had a full, bushy white beard. Freckles covered his face, hands and arms. His curious gaze rested on Jared as he greeted the others.

She took a deep breath while everyone greeted him in return, and then they all looked at her.

"Grandpa, this is my fiancé, Jared Whitewolf."

"Good golly, girl! You're marrying mighty suddenly. And a cowboy at that," he said, extending his hand to Jared, who shook with him.

"Grandpa!"

"That's all right," Jared said easily. "I am a cowboy. Glad to meet you, Mr. Kolanko."

"That's a big belt buckle. Looks like one of those prize buckles."

"It is, sir. Bull riding."

Grandpa leaned down to study Jared's buckle as if he was looking at his navel, and Faith shook her head. "Grandpa."

"World champion," he said, straightening to study Jared. "Have you won more than once?"

"Yes, sir."

"Do you love my granddaughter?"

"I asked her to be my wife."

"And you want to marry him?" Grandpa Morgan's green eyes bore into her.

"Yes, I do," she said firmly, feeling Jared's fingers tighten around hers.

"Are you pregnant, missy?"

A chorus of protests rose as she shook her head. "No."

"Then that sounds good enough. Means we'll get some tickets to a rodeo, doesn't it?" he asked Jared with a twinkle in his eye.

"Yes, sir. You could have gone last night if I had known

you might like to. There'll be another one in Tulsa about five months from now. You'll have tickets.''

"Good. Now, why all the sour faces around here?'' he asked.

"Dad, there are no sour faces,'' her father answered. "Faith's news is a surprise, that's all. Let's sit down.''

Jared sat in a chair near Faith and draped his arm across her shoulders, lightly playing with her shoulder while they talked, and she prayed her grandfather would not start asking questions about his mother and father.

In an hour they all went to the kitchen, where they ate sandwiches. Finally Faith felt they could escape. Before they finished their goodbyes, Faith had agreed to lunch with Meg on Monday and lunch with Andy on Tuesday. She could just imagine what the conversation would be both times.

When the pickup door closed and Jared started the motor, she fell back against the seat, doubts plaguing her. She looked at the house she had grown up in. Was she throwing away all stability and security and a happy future? She was marrying a cowboy who hadn't called any one place home in the past ten years. A drifter whose ambitions were centered on Merry and a family. Was she making a mistake?

"It'll be good,'' Jared said quietly, his fingers winding through hers.

"You're leaving town tomorrow,'' she remarked, still worrying about her decision.

"You're brave enough to deal with them without me. They love you and they want what's best for you. And at the moment it's difficult for them to think it's me.''

At the moment it was difficult for *her* to think it was him.

They rode in silence while her thoughts stormed. Her phone would be ringing when she got home and she would spend the next week trying to calm her family. And plan a wedding.

Will MacGiver's farm was east of Tulsa. As they reached

the fringe of the city and began to pass open fields, Jared abruptly pulled off on a dirt road.

"What's wrong?" she asked, suddenly afraid that her life was going to take yet another turn.

Seven

Jared didn't answer as he cut the engine, stepped outside, then walked around the pickup, a tall, lanky figure with moonlight spilling over his shoulders. His hat tilted to the back of his head, he opened her door and reached up to take her arm.

"Come here, Faith."

Her pulse jumped at the husky, determined tone of his voice, and she climbed down.

"I can feel your doubts like gale winds battering me," he said, sliding his arms around her waist. He leaned against the pickup and spread his legs, pulling her against him.

Her heart raced while indecision tore at her. Half of her wanted the engagement; half of her still resisted until she looked into his dark eyes and felt his arms around her. Tension flared, an almost tangible sizzle, as they looked into each other's eyes. The magic chemistry was there, urging her to tilt her mouth up to his.

His mouth brushed hers, warm, fleeting. Her heart thudded and heat flared low within her.

A new worry knocked on her door. He wasn't marrying her because he loved her. He *needed* her for Merry. Would he ever love her?

His tongue touched her lips and she quivered. His mouth was sure, seeking, seducing her senses. His arm tightened while his hand slid down her back over her bottom, pulling her closer against him. His thick manhood pressed against her, and her worries went up in smoke. She felt desired, womanly, needed. She was taking chances, running risks, and yet, this dangerous, wondrous man was as solid as a rock. She had seen the way he looked at Merry, the tenderness he poured out to her.

Faith Whitewolf. As she wound her arms tighter around him, she thought about his bloodlines, his ancestors who had roamed the land and lived by their strength and their wits. Maybe her family needed some of his risk-taking blood.

Jared ended the kiss abruptly and she opened her eyes. "That's better," he whispered. His hand slid from her shoulder down across her breasts. Her nipples tightened and she gasped with pleasure.

Jared wanted to pick her up, put her across the hood of the pickup and possess her, but he knew he had to go slow. They had to have a wedding first, and Faith had to be ready, to want him as much as he wanted her.

He slipped free the buttons of her blouse, his hands brushing aside the flimsy bra. He cupped her breasts and felt her quiver. Her hips thrust against him and her fingers threaded through his hair.

She was as soft as warm butter, her skin silken, and he wanted to feel her softness consume him. He wanted her beneath him, wanted to discover what would drive her to the height of passion, what would make her lose all her cool control.

Now wasn't the time or place, yet he had needed the

momentary intimacy as much as she had. The family gathering had been hell, but he could understand. Disapproval had steamed from her father and brothers. All evening Andy had looked on the brink of slugging him, and Jared didn't expect the man's anger to slack off until after the wedding. Someday he would be just as protective of Merry. He would probably be worse.

He bent, taking her nipple in his mouth, hearing a moan that threatened his iron control. It had been too damned long since he had been with a woman, and he was rapidly falling under the spell of this one. He was determined not to rush her, but it was straining every ounce of his restraint. He wanted her arms around him, wanted to hear her cry out his name. She was special, and every hour with her he wanted her more.

A motor registered in his mind and he realized a car was approaching. He straightened, pulled her blouse in place and held her close, turning her head against him so she couldn't be seen as twin headlights pierced the darkness and a car roared toward them.

While it swept past, he stroked her back, trying to let his body cool, but he was still pressed against her softness, still rock-hard with need.

"We better get Merry," she whispered, and moved away. He ached with wanting her as he walked around the pickup and climbed inside.

On Monday morning Faith reserved the church for the second of May, the first Saturday in the month. She had less than four weeks to plan the wedding. Jared had left town, but he called every night and they talked for hours. She was busy at work, busy with wedding plans and busy with getting the house ready. The time while Jared was away was taken up by her siblings, who were a divided camp, the males trying to talk her out of the marriage, Alice and Meg thinking it was wonderful.

But finally her wedding day dawned bright and sunny,

and as she got out of bed, she knew her life would change forever.

Faith stood in the dressing room of the church with Alice, Meg, and two of her best friends, Katie and Leah. Butterflies danced in her stomach while she thought of Jared. They had had so little time alone, but from this moment forward that would all change. She would be with him sometimes day and night.

Night.

Her pulse fluttered, and her thoughts skittered back to the wedding. Her bridesmaids were dressed in deep blue sleeveless dresses with straight skirts. She looked down at her white silk-and-satin dress without really seeing it.

She was going to marry Jared Whitewolf within the hour.

Doubts assailed her, and she wondered whether he was having last-minute jitters as well. She knew him well enough by now to suspect he had none. From their first meeting, he'd seemed determined to get to this destination.

"Faith, it's time," Meg announced. She crossed the room to straighten Faith's veil and brushed Faith's cheek with a kiss. "You're a beautiful bride."

"I think this is wonderful. I know you're going to be happy," Alice said, smiling.

When they left the dressing room, they found Andy standing in the hall. He strode to her, his walk purposeful, a scowl on his face. "Faith," he called to her, and she waved the others on, turning to her tall, blond brother, who looked handsome in his dark tuxedo.

"I thought you were ushering."

"There are other ushers," he said, pausing a few feet from her. "You can still get out of this."

"I don't want out, Andy."

"You don't love him."

"I'm doing what I want to do," she answered stiffly, knowing she couldn't put into words her motivations, or her feelings.

"I don't think he's in love with you. I can't figure it—why are the two of you doing this?"

"You've asked me before and I've told you before. We want to."

"Does he have some hold on you? Is there anything I can do?"

"No. I want to marry him," she replied firmly. "He wants to marry me. And we're not going to get married if I don't get out there."

"I think you're making a terrible mistake. He's not your type. He's all the things you don't know anything about. You're not into ranches and cowboys and cattle. And I know you're not one hundred percent sure of what you're doing. It shows, Faith. If you were falling all over him with stars in your eyes, I'd shut up, but you're not. I don't know why you're doing it, but it isn't about love."

"It's what I want."

"It can't be just to get a family, because Earl could have given you that. And would have. You were the one who broke it off. Dammit, you and Earl had far more in common than you and Hopalong."

"You have to stop referring to Jared as Hopalong," she said, losing her patience while Andy's scowl deepened.

"Hell, right now the guy's out there in boots and a tux."

"That's all right," she said through clenched teeth, clutching the bouquet of white roses and gardenias. "Andy, get out of my way."

They glared at each other. Her brother knew her too damned well. He probably could sense the qualms making her shake.

Reluctantly, he shook his head and stepped to one side. She swept past him. "Faith—"

She turned to look over her shoulder at him.

"I'll be there when you need me."

"Thanks, Andy. I know you will," she replied somberly, feeling a chilling foreboding.

"Faith," Meg called. "Andy, leave her alone! You're holding up the wedding."

"I'm going," he said.

"Our brother," Meg mumbled. "He can't understand how someone can fall in love with a person so entirely different. You're the only Kolanko to commit the sin, and it's beyond his comprehension. When a man loves a woman, it doesn't always matter about jobs and backgrounds."

Faith was quiet as she moved along the hall while Meg carried her train. Meg touched her arm. "Don't let Andy worry you. You're doing what you want. And you're marrying a man in love with you."

Faith wanted to cry out that he wasn't, but somehow Jared had Meg fooled.

Faith hurried to the foyer where her father studied her carefully. "Sure you want to do this?" he asked.

She nodded. "I'm sure," she said, feeling no such conviction, yet she was committed and she intended to marry.

They moved to the door as an organ flourish pealed in the air. And then they started down the aisle, and she looked at Jared who stood waiting at the altar.

Jared watched as Faith walked down the aisle toward him, and his certainty deepened a notch. This was *his* woman. Regal, poised, blond and beautiful. She was absolutely gorgeous, but the reason he had chosen her went far deeper than her looks. The woman was warm, caring, nurturing. She was efficient and intelligent, and he felt overwhelmed with his fortune in getting her to agree to marry him. He wanted this marriage to work.

When her green gaze met his, he could see her qualms. She looked pale, too solemn. He wanted to put his arms around her and reassure her that their life together would be good.

He wondered what she would think if she knew her father had offered him a sizable sum of money if he would pack up and disappear. He suspected her mother knew nothing about it. Nor did the others in the family. He was sure Andy wanted to beat him to a pulp, but in true Kolanko fashion, the man controlled himself. Keith probably felt the same. Only Meg and Alice were truly warm and friendly. Particularly Meg. He suspected she was glad to see her sister marry. And then there was Grandpa Kolanko. Jared thought he had the old man's approval.

He heard a soft coo and looked at Merry, who was in his grandmother's arms where they sat across from Faith's parents. Granddad caught Jared's eye and smiled.

Jared suspected Faith's parents were having difficulty adjusting to his Native American heritage, which showed so strongly in his grandparents. Wyatt and his family were seated in the row behind his grandparents, and Matt, looking as solemn as a judge, was seated next to Wyatt.

As Faith drew closer, Jared forgot about families. His bride was beautiful, and whether or not she loved him, he was going to relish the next moments. He hoped and expected that love would come to fill their lives.

When her father placed Faith's hand in his, Jared closed his hand gently around her icy fingers. Guilt stabbed him again that he had rushed her into this when she wasn't walking down the aisle starry-eyed and in love, but he would try to make it up to her. She raised her chin, and when they repeated their vows, her voice was strong and clear.

"I now pronounce you husband and wife."

The words were magical to Jared. He was married to this beautiful, wonderful woman, and he was going to do his best to make her fall in love with him.

Faith gazed up at her new husband. She had been dazed by him since that afternoon she met him and she still felt that way.

Husband and wife. She was *Mrs.* Jared Whitewolf. How had this happened so fast?

Jared lifted her veil, gently folding it behind her head. His actions were deliberate, his dark eyes holding her gaze.

He leaned down and brushed his warm lips across hers and then laced his fingers through hers as they turned to walk down the aisle to their future.

After the receiving line, the wedding party and family went back to the front of the church for pictures. Faith's mother and father hugged her. Meg gave her another hug. Even Andy wished her well.

Her uncle approached. "I wish you happiness, Faith. The whole office is still surprised."

"They'll adjust," she said, smiling as Blake kissed her cheek.

She turned to face Cornelia Whitewolf, who held out her arms. "Welcome to the Whitewolf family." She hugged Faith and stepped back. "Jared's our youngest grandchild—my baby. I'm so happy to see him married and settled. You'll be good for him, and both of you will be good for the little girl."

"Thank you, Cornelia," Faith said, turning to see Loughlan hand Merry to his wife and open his arms to hug Faith.

"Welcome to the family. Jared is blessed with you and Merry."

"I feel blessed, too," she answered.

"Faith, turn around and let's get your picture," Trey Holiday, the photographer, said. "Jared, get in the picture."

Much later, Jared's brothers wished her well. They were strangers to her, reminding her how little she knew her new husband.

The reception was held at her father's club, and guests spilled out onto the terrace and lawn until it was time for the first dance. When the moment arrived, Jared took her hand and led her to the dance floor.

"We've never even danced before," she said, realizing they should have practiced at least once. She had removed her train from her straight skirt. Jared placed his hand on her waist and held her other hand in his. She gazed into dark eyes filled with satisfaction, and they moved together as if they had danced a thousand times with each other. She forgot the reception, her family and guests. For the first time since she walked down the aisle, her nerves calmed and she felt sure.

When the dance ended, Jared asked her mother to dance and Faith danced with her father.

"I hope you're happy," he said quietly.

"Thank you. We plan to be."

"Just don't give up your job too fast. You've rushed into this marriage. Don't rush to change your entire life."

"You know I love my work," she answered, glancing past him at Jared. His hair was fastened behind his head and he looked handsome, this wild new husband of hers. Her mother was laughing at something he was telling her. His white teeth flashed, a contrast to his dark skin, and she longed to be dancing with him.

After they had cut the cake, Jared moved through the crowd that was largely Faith's guests. The few relatives he had had attended, but most of his friends were scattered across the country and few lived in Tulsa.

He turned to face Andy, who gazed at him solemnly. "Be good to her," the man said.

"I will be," Jared answered steadily. "She's very special."

Andy nodded, then moved away. Jared saw that his fists were clenched, and he wondered whether her brothers would ever approve of him.

Jared looked around the room, meeting Faith's gaze across the crowd. She was talking to friends, but watching him. They might as well have been alone as he stared back at her. He wanted to get the veil off her head and get her hair down.

"How's the groom?" Someone slapped him on the back and he turned to see Will MacGiver. His stocky, redheaded friend smiled at him.

"Glad to see a friend. Her family isn't falling over themselves with joy to see her marry a cowboy."

Will laughed. "She's the one who counts."

"Amen to that. That limo isn't due for another two hours, but I'm ready to get her and go."

"Patience, buddy. These shindigs are for the women. She's probably having the time of her life."

"I think I'll go see," Jared said, moving away.

The music changed to a fast number and Jared caught Faith's hand to lead her to the dance floor. In minutes he shed his coat and loosened his tie as he danced around her.

Faith couldn't take her gaze from the tall, sexy man she had married. He made her pulse race without doing anything more than looking at her. Sometimes just the sight of him set her heart fluttering.

It was late in the afternoon when they finally said their goodbyes to the family. Jared's grandparents were keeping Merry, allowing Faith and Jared to spend their week-long honeymoon alone.

They rushed to a waiting limousine. No sooner had they been seated, than they were whisked away. As they sped along the street, Faith felt a stab of panic. What had she done?

Jared slipped his arm around her, and she turned to look into his dark eyes.

He pulled her into his arms, his mouth covering hers in a long, possessive kiss that made her forget her surroundings, even the wedding. He shifted her to his lap, settling in the seat with his arms tightly around her while he kissed her. Wanting to be alone with him, she returned his kisses. They were husband and wife now. She wondered if it would ever cease to amaze her.

When his hand strayed lower, slipping down over her collarbone, she caught his wrist. "We're not alone."

Jared glanced beyond her at the driver and drew a deep breath, settling his hands on her waist while he looked at her. "Whatever you say, Mrs. Whitewolf."

The name sounded as if it should belong to someone else. She slid off his lap and straightened her dress as the limousine headed for the house on Peoria. They planned to change clothes and drive to the airport to fly to Colorado Springs, where Jared would compete in a rodeo that that evening.

When they arrived at the house, Jared carried her over the threshold, closing the front door with its oval of etched beveled glass with a kick of his foot. He locked the door and set her on her feet, tightening his arm around her waist as he leaned down to kiss her.

His kisses tempted her to toss aside her request for him to wait to consummate their hasty wedding. Excitement strummed across her nerves like a bow across fiddle strings. Mrs. Whitewolf. She was married. Falling in love.

The last thought brought her up short and she opened her eyes, looking up at him as she pushed away. Was she falling in love with this man?

"If you really want to ride in that rodeo, we better change clothes."

His dark eyes were filled with desire. He studied her solemnly, and she wondered whether he was going to forget the rodeo. He brushed his hand along her throat, a faint caress that made her ache for more.

"I'm signed up so I need to appear." He swung her into his arms and headed up the stairs.

"You don't need to carry me all the way upstairs," she said, her arms wrapped around his neck.

"You're a feather, darlin'. It's good exercise for me and I like carrying you," he answered easily as if holding her was an effortless feat.

At the top of the stairs, he crossed the hall into a bedroom. A four-poster mahogany bed was placed opposite a matching chest and mirror. He set her on her feet. A thick beige rug covered the middle of the room. Around its edges, the polished oak floor gleamed. Jared reached up to pull out pins and remove her veil.

"We have a few minutes, and I've been wanting to do this since you walked down the aisle."

"I'm glad you waited," she said, watching him, his dark
eyes on her while he pulled pins out of her hair. "You're
ruining a very expensive hairdo."

"Do you care?"

"No," she whispered, finding his steady gaze as tor-
menting as his caresses. His eyes smoldered with longing.
She felt fluttery inside, wanting him, and yet all her caution
urged her to wait because they were strangers in so many
ways.

Locks tumbled over her shoulders, and Jared could feel
his desire escalating. Her lips parted, red from his kisses
already. Her eyes were languorous, sexy. He wanted to peel
her out of the wedding dress and make love to her and
forget the rodeo, but he wasn't going to do it. They had
made an agreement about this marriage. As far back as he
could remember, he had satisfied his body's yearnings
when he wanted. This time, he was going to practice control. He wanted a lot more than her body. He wanted her
love.

He stepped back. "I'll change. We have to leave as soon
as we can for the airport or we'll miss that plane."

Faith watched him go, closing the door behind him. She
hadn't wanted him to stop kissing her, but she knew it was
best that he did. All along she had told herself that she
wanted to know him better before they fully became man
and wife, but she was changing her mind swiftly.

She kicked off her satin pumps and began to unfasten
the tiny row of buttons down her back. When she couldn't
reach the buttons in the middle, she started from the bottom
and worked her way up.

She still couldn't reach the middle buttons, and a glance
at the clock indicated that in a few more minutes Jared
would be ready and waiting. Biting her lip, she rushed
down the hallway. Even though his door stood open, she
knocked.

"Come in," he called.

She stepped inside the bedroom she had decorated in

bright maroon, hunter's green and white with a king-size four-poster mahogany bed, a chintz-covered love seat and a thick carpet in the center of the room. Jared straightened from rummaging in the closet. He gave a jerk to his head, shaking his shaggy black hair away from his face. It swirled across his shoulders, giving him that wild look she remembered from their first meeting. He was in his stocking feet, a pair of boots in hand. He was bare-chested, in jeans that were only partially buttoned.

"I can't get this dress unbuttoned," she said, staring at his chest. Smooth, brown skin was taut over powerful muscles. A few thin, pale scars slashed across his ribs and chest and shoulder. His stomach was flat, a washboard of muscles, and just above the vee of his jeans she saw a white band of what must be low-cut briefs.

He dropped the boots, and when her gaze flew up to meet his she realized how she had been studying him. His eyes filled with dark secrets she couldn't fathom, he crossed the room.

Jared drew a deep breath. "Turn around," he said in a husky voice. Her blatant perusal had sent his temperature soaring, and as he looked at her slender back, he felt on fire. She wasn't wearing a bra, and he could see her white lacy bikinis, the luscious curve of her bottom. He wanted to trail his tongue over her bare back, slide his hands around beneath the dress and haul her up against him.

Instead, he knew he better hold to his rodeo agenda. But it wasn't going to hurt to get in a few kisses. He leaned down to brush his mouth across her nape and heard her swift intake of breath. He took his own sweet time with the four remaining buttons, trailing his fingers across her back and down to the first button.

"Jared," she whispered.

His tongue flicked over her ear and he untwisted another button. He trailed his tongue across her shoulder, down over her back. She tilted her head back, and he leaned forward enough to see that her eyes were closed.

He twisted free another button and then the last. Before he released her, he slid his hands beneath the dress, letting one hand go around her waist and the other slide down, following the curve of her bottom.

She moaned and turned as his hand cupped her breast and his thumb flicked over her nipple. She reached out to trail her hands over his chest.

Faith hurt with a need that came to life forcefully. She raised her face and his mouth came down over hers. As their tongues tangled, she could feel his manhood hard against her stomach. His hand caressed her bottom as he pulled her up tighter against him.

How long did they kiss? Minutes or seconds? She twisted away. "You'll miss your rodeo."

Jared didn't give a damn, but he was going to wait. He had to try to win her affections. Otherwise, he felt certain the lady would be gone from his life.

Reluctantly, he released her, watching as she pulled her dress up. Her gaze raked over him, and he knew she could see the effect she had on him. She turned swiftly and left the room.

Jared wondered how long he could take this. Each time he held her in his arms, it pushed him closer to an edge where control vanished. He wanted her desperately, and he knew he was going to have sleepless nights and an aching body.

With a pounding heart, Faith rushed down the hall to dress. She wanted to be in Jared's arms, in his bed. She also wanted his love.

But words of love had never crossed his lips. And once she gave herself to him, she might be hopelessly lost—unable to love anyone else. Don't rush into it, she warned herself.

She drew a deep breath, thinking about the bargain she had gotten herself into. Would they ever fall in love? And if they didn't—should she rush to his bed? She wanted a baby of her own. And she felt Jared was holding back because he had promised her he would. Yet, like her, she sensed he was vulnerable to hurt. Was he trying to be cautious, too?

Knowing that time was precious, she dressed in new jeans that fit like a second skin, a red Western shirt, and she pulled on snakeskin boots that Jared had given her. She brushed her hair, knowing he liked it down over her shoulders. The reflection in the mirror seemed to be that of a stranger. Was it really her wearing tight jeans and boots?

"Ready?" Jared called.

Her body still ached for him and she was more than ready to start their life together. She picked up her purse and hurried into the hall.

He stood at the foot of the stairs. His hair was fastened behind his head again and he was picking up the carry-ons and his hat.

"Here I come," she said, rushing down the stairs. He glanced up, then dropped everything he was holding. He straightened and placed his hands on his hips as his gaze drifted over her.

"What?" she asked, stopping on the third step.

He came forward, fire dancing in his dark eyes. His hands went to her waist, then slid down to her thighs. "You are one good-looking woman."

"I feel half-naked in these tight jeans."

"I'll admit I'd rather keep you at home where no one can see you except me."

"That's ridiculous," she said, her cheeks turning pink as she descended the last steps.

Jared clenched his fists and jammed his hat on his head. Then he picked up the bags and carry-ons to avoid reaching for her. She rushed past him and he watched the switch of her hips, remembering when he had run his hand over her soft, round bottom.

His body was reacting to her as if he was fifteen years old and had never seen a woman. "Dammit," he muttered, and followed her out to the pickup. As she climbed in, he couldn't resist. He reached out, his hand following the curve of her jeans across her bottom. She glanced over her shoulder at him, a seductive, flirtatious look on her face, and then she sat in the pickup.

He grinned as she leaned in the open window. "You're irresistible, Mrs. Whitewolf."

Faith's pulse jumped. He acted as if he wanted her, yet he always stopped. But wasn't she the one who had asked him to stop? And wasn't he the one who had given her his promise that he would wait? So what did she really want him to do?

Hours later, they arrived at Colorado Springs and stood outside in a cool, crisp late afternoon waiting for the shuttle to take them to the rental car. Shuttles, taxis, buses and cars drove past while a crowd milled on the walk and people crossed the busy lanes of traffic.

Faith saw a mother turn to fix a broken strap on her suitcase. Her towheaded toddler, green ball in hand, wiggled free and climbed out of her stroller. The ball rolled away from the child and she toddled after it. The little girl could only be about eighteen months old, Faith guessed, thinking of how Merry would look at that age.

People moved in front of Faith, and she lost sight of the mother and toddler, but then she glimpsed the child's red sunsuit...and she saw the green ball roll into the street. Frozen with horror, Faith stared as the child toddled after her ball, oblivious of oncoming vehicles.

"Jared—" Faith started to run.

Someone yelled and a horn blared.

But Jared was already gone, dashing headlong into the lanes after the toddler.

Eight

Faith felt as if her heart stopped beating when Jared dodged a bus and snatched up the child as a shuttle slammed on its brakes and skidded toward her.

As the shuttle rocked to a stop, Jared rushed back to the sidewalk. The mother took her child, holding her and crying while a man asked Jared if he was all right.

Faith stared at him, knowing that she had married a man of action. He would always rush into things. And he was a man who didn't stop to think about the danger involved. Was she going to be able to cope with a daredevil who threw caution to the winds?

Jared returned to her side. "There's our shuttle," he said, pointing past her. She glanced around to see the blue-and-gold shuttle waiting at the curb.

As soon as they boarded, Jared flung their bags on a shelf and sat down beside her. He glanced her way, but said nothing.

At the car rental agency, she stood outside in the hot

sunshine and waited while he made arrangements for the car. She watched him through the glass as he leaned against the counter. He looked relaxed, as if the incident and any effects from it were over.

He didn't speak until much later, when they were settled in the rental car.

"Why so quiet?" he asked.

"My nerves are still vibrating." She twisted in the seat to look at him. "Do have any nerves in your body? Are you afraid of anything?"

Afraid of losing you ran through his mind. Jared kept his eyes on the road. "You're angry because I dashed out into traffic."

"I'm not angry. I just don't know whether I can live with someone who is constantly throwing himself into danger."

"You do every day when you drive to work. The freeway isn't the safest place to be. Besides that, you had already started running toward her. If I hadn't been there, darlin', I know who would have been out in front of traffic."

"I don't know whether I would have or not. But I'm not just reacting to what happened today. Bull riding, the broncs. When a crisis happens, you're right in the middle of things."

"Someone needs to be," he answered solemnly. "And you were already on your way. I recall you charging through the bushes at the park to rescue Merry, so it's the pot calling the kettle black."

"Maybe," she replied, still thinking how close he had come to being struck by the shuttle bus. "I'm thankful you saved the little girl."

"Then don't worry. That's the first time in my life anything like that has ever happened and let's hope it's the last."

"But I'll bet you've waded into fights. I'll bet you'll do dangerous things when you own your ranch."

"Our ranch. Are we fighting?" he asked, picking up her hand to brush his lips across her knuckles. His breath was warm, his fingers locked through hers were firm. She gazed into his dark eyes and shook her head.

"No, because I might have run out there if you hadn't. The little girl would have been hit by the shuttle if you hadn't scooped her up. It just made me wonder again whether I can cope with your way of living."

"Believe me, darlin', you can."

His words came back later to haunt her as she watched a large Brahman bull bound out of the chute with Jared clinging to it. She closed her eyes, listening to the crowd, unable to look again until the buzzer sounded. She watched Jared jump on the fence out of the way of the charging bull. Would she ever grow accustomed to the wild side of him?

Early in the last ride the bull rider was tossed, but his hand was caught in the rope and the bull flung him around like a rag doll. She'd closed her eyes, feeling a knot in her stomach. The crowd had become quiet, and then a collective sigh went up from the audience. Only then had she opened her eyes. The clowns had chased the bull from the arena while men knelt over the rider, who lay motionless in the dirt. Time passed, and more men went out to look at the inert cowboy. Over the loudspeaker the master of ceremonies announced they were clearing the way for an ambulance. Watching the terrifying scene unfold, she had thought how devastated she would feel if it was Jared on the ground.

Had she made a mistake? Tying her life to a man who was accustomed to violence and action? Every time doubts rose, all she had to do was think of the quiet moments with him, times he had been with Merry, and then she felt confident she had done the right thing.

When Jared made his way to the box, she could see his

concern for her on his face as his dark eyes searched hers. "Okay?"

"I need to ask you that." She couldn't keep from reaching for him. She saw the startled flicker in his eyes, and then his arms went around her and he hugged her.

"I'm fine. Actually, I won the bull riding."

His shirt smelled like leather and cotton, a fragrance she suspected she would associate with him forever. He released her to look at her again and she smiled, relieved the rodeo was over for the night.

"C'mon," he said. "It's time to eat and see that you have some fun."

They went to a rustic restaurant with a group of his friends. The music was loud, and when Jared took her hand to dance, she shook her head. "I don't know the two-step."

"It's just like it sounds, and incredibly easy. Here, look." He showed her the steps and she watched his dusty black boots move through the basic dance. Then he took her hand to lead her to the dance floor. After the first few steps, she realized it was easy and she moved with him, her gaze locked with his as she remembered the dance they'd shared during their wedding, which had only been hours before—not the lifetime ago that it seemed.

After the slow number for the two-step, the band broke into a foot-stomping fast number and Jared whirled her about the dance floor. His hat was pushed to the back of his head, and his hair was untied and hanging loose. He grinned as he spun her around until he was in such a sweat that he popped the snaps on the front of his shirt down to his waist.

As they danced, Faith couldn't help but look at his bare chest that was damp with sweat. Virile, sexy—he lived life with a zest that she had never experienced. Was he going to be *too* wild for her? Would she be too tame for him?

She'd noticed how women flirted with him all evening, but he'd been casually cool and kept his arm around Faith's shoulders, carefully introducing her to everyone as his bride.

It was in the early hours of the morning that they returned to their hotel. Jared had gotten adjoining rooms. He unlocked her door, stepped inside and pulled her into his arms to kiss her. The minute his mouth met hers, she melted. Always, in his arms, her doubts went up in smoke, burned away by kisses that made her ache for more.

When he released her, she was breathless. She wanted to pull him closer, yet she was uncertain about his feelings. Gazing up at him, she tried to decide what he really felt for her.

"This is our wedding night, but we made an agreement and I'll stick by it," he said quietly, caressing her throat, his fingers lingering, moving to trail across her nape. Tingles radiated from his touch and she was already on fire from his kisses. She wanted to tell him she was ready to toss aside her request to wait before they consummated the marriage, yet she felt uncertain.

He brushed a light kiss across her lips, then turned and left, closing the door to his room behind him. She stared at the closed door, half tempted to go after him.

She lay in bed that night and felt alone, too aware Jared was only feet away. Was he soundly asleep? She suspected he was, suffering none of the desire he had ignited in her. All she had to do was get up and go into his room and she could end this waiting period that was of her own making. At the same time, the caution that she had practiced her entire life warned her to take her time and be sure what she wanted. They were married, but it was in name only, something she needed to remember.

Restless, she got up and went to sit by the window, gazing outside at city lights, remembering Jared's kisses, his eyes on her all during their wedding ceremony, the moments in his bedroom later.

It was over an hour before she climbed back into bed

and lay staring into the darkness, still too aware he was asleep only yards away from her.

The next couple of days were uneventful, and on Tuesday they arrived home to a quiet house. Faith looked at the new furniture, the few things she had brought from her apartment. The big living area was rustic, comfortable. She had decorated it in a way that she hoped he would like. The polished floor gleamed and furniture was large and comfortable with a deep-green-and-beige color scheme. The walls were bare, the mantel bare—they would add things after they had lived here awhile. Although she'd placed some of her books on the bookshelves, she realized Jared had very few possessions other than his pickup and saddle and clothing. The house was silent except for the scrape of Jared's boots on the floor.

"I'll grill steaks and we can sit outside. It'll cool when the sun goes down."

She went upstairs to shower, changing to cutoffs and a red T-shirt. When she stepped outside, Jared was standing at the grill. He had a beer in one hand, a long fork in the other. He had shed his shirt and was bare-chested.

He turned and looked at her, his gaze drifting over her legs and then back up to her face. His dark brow arched. "Wow. I haven't seen you in shorts before," he said, looking at her legs again.

"The feeling is mutual," she answered, and his dark eyes flicked to hers as he gave her a probing stare. They had been married four days now, and in those four days the tension between them had built. He constantly touched her, brushed against her, kissed her often. Her nerves were raw, her awareness of him continuing to heighten while she debated whether to toss caution aside and tell him she was ready to be man and wife in every way.

Her gaze slid over his muscled back as he turned meat on the grill. In spite of his daredevil life-style and his strong will, she knew Jared had a vulnerable side. Growing up, he had been hurt, and she didn't want to add another hurt.

Nor did *she* want to get hurt. Once she took their relationship to the next step, she feared the consequences. She might never be able to accept anything less than his love. And he might never fall in love with her.

She moved farther away from him, touching the flatware he had set on the table. This night, she would cling to caution; it was too soon to consummate their shaky marriage.

They spent the rest of the week looking at land since Faith was still on vacation. On Sunday morning, they drove to Anadarko and out to the farm to get Merry, spending a day with Jared's grandparents and then starting back to Tulsa in the evening. They got home long after midnight and tucked Merry into her tiny bed in the small nursery that adjoined the master bedroom.

During the middle of the night, Faith awakened to hear Merry screaming. She shoved away the sheet and rushed to Merry's room. As she stepped inside, Jared was already picking her up. He wore low-cut white briefs and nothing else. The faint glow of the night-light highlighted the curve of solid muscles. She became aware of herself, of the T-shirt that was all she was wearing.

He jiggled Merry and then turned, looking at Faith. "You take her and try to calm her. I don't know what's wrong."

She took Merry from him and paced, speaking softly. In seconds, when Merry quieted, Faith looked around. Jared had gone, but he returned wearing his jeans.

"You have a magic touch. What do you think is wrong?"

"Your grandmother thinks she might be getting a new tooth. Maybe that's all it was."

He leaned against the doorjamb and she was aware of his dark eyes studying her. "Want me to take her?"

"I don't mind. Besides, I think she's gone back to sleep," she said, holding Merry away to look at her. Smoky lashes sparkling with unshed tears fanned over her full, rosy cheeks. "She's asleep." Faith carried her to the bed and leaned over to put her down.

Jared stood watching Faith, the T-shirt pulling across her bottom with each step. When she leaned over the baby crib, her shirt hiked up. He drew a deep breath at the view of her long legs. The shirt covered her bottom. Barely. But his imagination whisked it away.

She straightened and crossed the room. The shirt was loose and her breasts bounced slightly as she walked. She looked disheveled from bed, feminine, alluring. Together, they walked into the darkened hall that had only a faint light from the bedroom and a shaft of light from her open door.

"Faith," he said, his voice husky. His pulse pounded, and he couldn't resist reaching for her, his arm sliding around her waist. He pulled her close. The shirt was the only thing she was wearing and he could feel her warm, soft body.

Sweat popped out as if he was in a sauna. He leaned down to kiss her. The moment his mouth covered hers, their tongues touching, his roaring pulse drowned out all other sounds. The world shifted beneath him, desire sweeping him on a rushing current. With a hunger that threatened to consume him, he kissed her and molded her body to his.

Each time they held each other and kissed, he knew they were moving closer to consummation. His bride was sexy, adorable and so good with Merry. Faith was all he wanted, and he ached to take her to his bed and discover her secret pleasures. He wanted to make wild, passionate love with her, but he had to remember the stakes. While he was becoming desperate for her body, he wanted so much more. He wanted the lady's love and rushing her to bed might cause him to lose her.

Faith clung to him, knowing the first buttons of his jeans

were unfastened. She remembered him standing in his briefs, his firm buttocks outlined clearly. He leaned away from her now, his hands sliding slowly up over her rib cage, moving beneath the T-shirt to cup her breasts. She gasped with pleasure, forgetting theirs was a marriage of convenience, forgetting everything except his hands and the strong man caressing her.

She hadn't known it could be this way between a man and a woman. She had never been turned to a quivering mass of boneless jelly before, never wanted a man with a craving that blocked out rational thought. She trailed her fingers over his chest, down across his stomach.

Jared shoved the T-shirt higher and paused to look at her body, bared to his view. He inhaled deeply, trying to hang on to his control. Rosy skin, pink nipples, golden hair, lush curves and a slender body. He palmed a breast, its softness having the opposite result on him. Rock hard, he wanted her. He bent to flick his tongue over her nipple.

Faith's fingers bit into his arms, feeling firm muscles while pleasure raked her. The ache low in her body intensified. She wanted his loving, was more than ready for him. Her hands trailed across his smooth, powerful chest while her heart thudded.

He took a nipple in his mouth, biting so lightly, then curling his tongue around the taut peak. She gasped and twisted, her hips thrusting toward him, but he shifted, his hand sliding to the juncture of her thighs, spreading her legs slightly, searching in the soft curls.

"Jared, please—" she whispered, knowing there was a huge void in her life that only he could fill. This strong man was exciting, virile, sexy enough to turn her to quaking mush. Why was she waiting?

His hand moved, finding her hot, honeyed center, stroking her. Jared watched her through hooded eyes as she tensed. Her hips moved frantically, and while he caressed and rubbed her, her fingers dug into him. Her lower lip was caught in her white teeth, her eyes were closed and her head was thrown back, the golden mane of hair hanging over her back. She was lost in a frenzy of passion and he was going to lose his control. He couldn't get his breath and his heart thudded violently against his rib cage.

"Jared, your bed." Even though she whispered, he heard her words.

He felt as if he might explode. His body throbbed, hammering for release, wanting her beyond anything he had dreamed possible. Faith was going up in flames, hips wildly moving while she clung to him as if for life, whispering what she wanted.

"Jared, please—" She was wet, hot, ready for him, but he wanted her heart ready and aching with a need that would begin to match his.

A spasm rocked her and Faith gasped for breath as she arched against him. "Jared," she whispered again, tugging on his arms. His arms wrapped around her, crushing breath from her lungs as he kissed her deeply. She could feel him trembling. He was covered in sweat, and she knew he was having as strong a response as she was, yet he was sticking to their bargain. He picked her up and carried her to her room, setting her on her feet.

Her body pulsed with need for him, need for completion. She no longer cared about marriage agreements. She wanted him, and he had to know it. She clutched his upper arms.

"I want to stay. God knows, I want to stay with you, Faith. But we made a bargain and I made a promise that I intend to keep." His voice was a husky rasp, while his midnight eyes devoured her.

He turned swiftly and left her room, closing the door. Fighting the urge to run after him, to throw herself at him, she sat down. Her body throbbed. She was ready; she did not want to wait any longer. She stood and crossed the room, her hand on the knob, and then she paused. *He doesn't love me* ran through her mind. Yet she knew how he'd trembled when he held her and kissed her. He felt *something*.

Sitting on the bed, she wrapped her arms around her drawn-up knees. She ached for his loving, and for his love. It would come with time, she told herself, but that was little consolation now. She closed her eyes and could see him standing holding Merry, wearing only his briefs. She groaned, knowing sleep would be long in coming tonight.

The next morning, she woke, dressed and found Jared with breakfast waiting and Merry happily in her baby carrier while he spoon-fed her baby food.

"My goodness, this is service I'm not accustomed to before going to work. I usually just drink juice and eat toast," she said, looking at the bowl of fresh fruit, the orange juice that was poured and the toast he had buttered. "How's our little girl?" she asked, brushing a kiss on Merry's head.

"She's none the worse for the night. She fared better than I did. I'm taking her with me to look at some property today. We'll go to the gym—"

"You take this baby to a gym?"

"Sure. They have a sitter for little ones. I have to stay in shape for the circuit. Use it or lose it."

"I don't think you're in any danger of losing it," she remarked dryly, and he grinned. "I should be home by six."

Faith leaned against the counter to drink her juice, watching Jared feed Merry. There was a cozy intimacy to sharing the morning with him. She relished it, thinking of her lonely nights and rushed mornings before their marriage. Merry looked adorable, diligently taking each offered bite, her blue eyes on Jared. And Faith didn't blame her. He was worth watching. One long leg was propped on a knee as he leaned across the table to feed her. He wore jeans and a T-shirt and his hair hung loose around his face. He shook it away and glanced at her, arching his brows as he caught her studying him. "Remembering last night, I hope?" he asked quietly.

She inhaled. "Maybe, but I better get my thoughts on work."

His gaze flicked over her, and she became aware of her appearance, the straight red skirt and her white blouse.

"You look great. If you're not afraid of mashed bananas getting spit on you, come here."

"I think I better give the little lady plenty of room," she said, worrying more about what would happen if she let him hug and kiss her.

He set down the small jar of mashed bananas and stood, his gaze locked with Faith's as he crossed the room to her. He slid his hand behind her head.

"Am I going to have to change because of wrinkles?"

"I wouldn't think of causing you to wrinkle," he answered, leaning forward to kiss her. The only contact was his hand on her nape, but every inch of her body came alive, quivering with awareness of the last time he had touched her. As his tongue slowly stroked hers, delving into her mouth, stirring her response, she slid her arms around his neck.

"I can't resist you," she whispered, her mouth moving against his. Dimly she heard Merry babbling and beginning to fuss.

He pulled away to study her. "That's a good start to the day." He turned back to feed Merry, and Faith felt her nerves quivering and little fires building inside her. She drew a deep breath and forgot about breakfast, rushing past him to collect her things and get out of the house before she threw herself at him.

She hadn't been at work an hour when her uncle called her into his office. As soon as she was seated across the desk from Blake, he smiled at her.

"You look like the beautiful new bride. How's married life?"

"Very nice."

"Good. Now, let's talk about life here in the office. Faith, we're so pleased with the work you've been doing. I think you're a real asset to this office."

"Thank you," she said, feeling a twinge of guilt because she hadn't given a thought to her job for well over a week now.

"And because of the accounts you have helped us to get this year and the way our clients like your work, I think it's time we promoted you. Porter also deserves to move up. He will become vice president of accounts. You will take his place as vice president of design."

"My word! This is really a surprise," she said honestly, not expecting a promotion like the one she was receiving for another few years. "I'm thrilled! I didn't expect anything like this."

He smiled and talked about her new position while her mind wandered to the thought of telling Jared. And she realized that her new husband was going to be less than thrilled. Shoving aside the worries that had cropped up, she tried to concentrate on what Blake was saying.

By noon everyone in the office was congratulating her. As soon as she had left Blake's office, she called Jared, but no one answered and she remembered he was going to look at property. She dreaded telling him the news. She knew he wouldn't be impressed with her raise, and the promotion would tie her more closely than ever to her work.

Just before she left for lunch with her close friend, Katie, she paused at a window. She looked out over the treetops and grassy area beyond and the wide blue-gray ribbon of the Arkansas River, the tall smokestacks of the refineries and the industrial area beyond it. Where was Jared and when would he be home? Was he going to hate her new promotion? She remembered how nothing ever seemed to bother him, but she suspected this might.

And she had to give thought to her own reaction. Her

priorities were changing. And, she realized, Jared's feelings about her work were becoming important.

Beneath bright sunshine, Jared walked beside the Realtor. High grass swished against his legs. He looked out over the expanse of land stretching away from the house and drew a deep breath. The land was rolling, covered in high green grass. An occasional tall cottonwood stood against the horizon and trees lined the creek that meandered three hundred yards from the house.

He glanced at the house. Weeds grew to the door. Shingles had peeled away from the roof. Screens were missing from broken windows and weathered boards needed painting, but the basic structure would be sound if it had a new roof. Made of brick and wood, the long ranch-style house had an overhang above a porch that ran the length of the house. The agent, Jim Creighton, unlocked the door and motioned to Jared to enter.

"The house needs work, but the buyer will get the land at a bargain rate because the estate wants to sell and they don't want to wait. The house can be torn down and another one built, for that matter. You'll save enough on the land. Everything around here costs more than this place."

Merry played with a rattle, and Jared carried her easily as he walked into the living room and looked at the large stone fireplace, the wide-plank floor and the empty built-in oak bookshelves that flanked the fireplace. He wandered from room to room, and he could imagine the place repaired and he could see Faith, Merry and himself living in it. The rooms were large, with four big bedrooms and three baths. Along the living area was a window that gave a panoramic view of the sloping land to the south.

"I'd like to bring my wife out to look at it," he said, relishing talking about Faith. The word *wife* was still new and unique to him, something he had never before applied to himself, but now every time he said it, he smiled.

"Sure. What time is convenient?" Creighton asked, getting out a small black notebook and opening it to write down the time.

"Tonight should be fine. It'll stay light until late. How about eight o'clock?"

Creighton gave Jared a key and told him to look when he wanted and get back with him. They locked up and Jared told the agent goodbye, saying he was going to stay to look around. As soon as the agent had driven away, Jared got into his pickup with Merry and drove across the land behind the house. He found tracks and followed them, driving over the property until he had satisfied himself that he had found the ranch he wanted.

He couldn't wait to show it to Faith.

The minute Faith walked through the door that night, Jared caught her up in his arms and swung her around. She laughed, and as he let her slide down the length of him, her smile vanished. She tilted her head and closed her eyes when he kissed her. Her heart raced and thoughts of work vanished. Finally she leaned away to look up at him. "You look happy."

"I am. I found us a ranch today."

"No! You bought land?"

"'Course not. I want you to see it and see what you think," he said, nuzzling her neck.

"I won't know one thing about buying a ranch. Where's Merry?"

"Sound asleep. She likes the place."

"Oh, I'm sure. Merry always loves the things her daddy does."

"That she does, darlin'."

"Where is this ranch?"

"That's one of the good things. Only a stone's throw out of town. I can get back and forth easily, and we can live right here for a long time."

Faith remembered her promotion, but she knew she should hear him out about the ranch first. He sounded pleased, and she wondered if it was as close as he said. And every time he talked about how easy it would be for him to get from Tulsa to a nearby ranch, she wondered if what was really on his mind was her working on a ranch and coming into town a couple of times a week to an office.

"I have the key, and I thought we'd go look at the place, then I'll take you to dinner."

"That sounds like a bribe."

"Nope. I can do better than that if I want to bribe you," he drawled, his tongue following the curve of her ear. Faith inhaled, trying to concentrate on their conversation, feeling she had been away from him for days instead of hours. "If you don't like the place, I'll keep looking. The house is a shambles, but it looks as if it can be fixed up to be real livable. And I promise to put in a new kitchen."

"That sounds ominous. A new kitchen means very bad shape."

"Maybe so, but it has great possibilities. I can always see the great possibilities," he said, raining warm kisses down to the vee of her blouse. She could smell the woodsy after-shave he wore, feel his warm breath on her, and it was difficult to keep her thoughts on the concerns of the day.

"Jared, I was promoted today to vice president," she said breathlessly, barely thinking about the consequences as she felt his fingers twist the top button of her blouse free.

He straightened to look down at her. "You should have told me when you came in. Congratulations! That's fantastic."

"I was afraid you wouldn't be happy about it."

"If that pleases you, then it suits me just fine, darlin'. I'm not surprised. You have to be the best talent they have."

She felt as if a weight had been lifted from her shoulders. He seemed genuinely happy for her, and for the first time since she had learned about the promotion, she felt really thrilled about it. "You mean it?"

"I mean it," he said with warmth in his dark eyes. "And we'll take Merry and go celebrate your promotion. We can look at the ranch site tomorrow night."

"Oh, no, we can't. Uncle Blake told Dad about my promotion, and Dad's having a celebration for me tomorrow night. It'll be dinner at his club with the whole family, close friends and some of the office people. So we can go look at the ranch tonight when Merry wakes up."

"Congratulations again, Faith. That is really great."

"Thank you," she said, looking up at him, feeling drawn into the depths of his dark eyes where magic wrapped around her and shut out the cares of the day. She stood on tiptoe and wound her arms around his neck and he leaned down to kiss her.

Merry's cries caused them to move away and Jared turned, striding across the room. "I'll get her. You change and we'll go out."

The phone rang and Faith picked it up to hear Meg's voice.

"Congratulations! I've heard from Dad about your promotion! That's fantastic."

"Thanks, Meg."

"Bet Jared thinks it's great, too."

"Yes, he does."

"I thought you two might want to celebrate before the family shindig tomorrow night. Would you like to bring Merry over here so you two can be alone?"

"That sounds great, but Merry doesn't know any of you."

"She knows us a little from the wedding, and she's going to get to know us plenty."

"Umm, let me ask Jared."

"Ask Jared what?" he asked, strolling back into the room with a teary-eyed, tousled baby in his arms. He got her bottle from the refrigerator and Merry reached for it as he uncapped it and placed it in the microwave briefly.

"Meg offered to keep Merry tonight while we celebrate."

"If that pleases you, then it suits me just fine, darlin'," he drawled, capping the bottle after the timer sounded while balancing Merry on one hip. The baby grabbed the bottle and jammed it into her mouth. "You know she likes to be with other children, so if Meg is up to it, okay."

"Fine. You have a deal, Meg. We'll keep yours in return."

"I had a method to my madness. Bring her any time."

Jared took the phone from Faith. "Thanks, sister-in-law."

"Any time."

He handed the phone to Faith, then pulled out the pins in her hair so it fell over her shoulders while she talked. His fingers brushed her neck lightly, then touched her cheek while he stood close enough that she could feel the warmth of his body.

"And Merry can stay tomorrow night, too," Meg said. "Stan's mom will be here, and she'll look after the kids while we're at the party. How's that?"

Faith inhaled deeply as Jared's finger slipped beneath her collar, gliding lightly over the curve of her breast.

"Faith?"

Startled, she realized Meg was still talking. "Right. I better go. Thanks a million, Meg." She replaced the phone and turned to catch his hand in hers. "I can't talk when you do things like that." She leaned closer to Merry. "Hello, sweetie. I missed you today."

Glancing up at Jared, she held out her hands. "You've had her all day. Can I have her now?"

He handed Merry over. The baby stopped drinking to smile at Faith, squealing in delight, and Faith felt something squeeze her heart.

Warmth and love enveloped her for the small baby in her arms. "Oh, Jared, I love her so!"

He smiled and rubbed his knuckles on Faith's cheek. "She probably fell in love with you that afternoon you came to her rescue."

"I love you, sweet thing. You're my little girl now," she said, heading toward the family room and the new rocking chair.

Jared watched her, feeling a deep yearning. Would she ever look at him with the same tenderness in her eyes that she bestowed on Merry?

An hour later, Faith had showered and changed to jeans and a T-shirt. They left Merry at Meg's and Jared drove southeast out of the city. While he drove, he told her details about the ranch. "It just came on the market, Faith."

"Why are they selling at such a reduced price?"

"The couple who owned it left it to their only daughter, who has ignored it for about a year. She lives in England, cares nothing about the ranch and simply wants to be rid of it."

The pickup ran over a rickety bridge above a dry creek bed. "We'll have to replace this bridge."

"I don't know why. There's no water in the creek."

"There will be when the next big rains come. I know how these creeks can fill up to become raging torrents where before there'd been nothing but dirt." He drove up to the house that was bathed in the early evening rays of the setting sun.

Faith gazed at a rambling ranch house of weathered wood with a porch along the front. Shingles were missing from the roof, and the porch rail had fallen to the ground and was half-hidden by weeds.

"Jared, it looks like it needs a lot of work," she said, appalled by the run-down condition of the place.

"We can get it done," he said cheerfully. "It's structurally sound except for the roof. Come look at it."

Faith walked beside him, trying to concentrate on the house and land, far more aware of the man at her side. His arm was across her shoulders, and he kept her close against him until they had finished their tour.

It was almost dark when he leaned back against the pickup and pulled her around to face him. "Want to buy it?"

"Just like that?" She laughed. "Shouldn't we look around at other places? You rush into everything."

"Only things I want to rush into. Only very special deals," he said, his dark eyes working their magic on her senses.

"I don't know anything about ranches. The house is all right. But I think you should look around some more. This is a big decision." She rubbed her forehead. "I might as well save my breath. You rushed into marriage. You're going to plunge into this."

"I'm not rushing anywhere. I think I'm showing impressive restraint," he said, and Faith wondered whether he was talking about the ranch or about making love to her. His fingers stroked her nape while his other hand slid down over her bottom in a casual, feathery stroke.

"Jared, do what you want," she said, knowing he would, anyway.

"It involves you, too. This will wipe out that net worth of mine. I'll have to take out a loan."

She looked up at him, touching his jaw, feeling the faint stubble. "I have savings you can have."

"Thank you, darlin'," he replied warmly. "You keep your savings. You might need it sometime. I'll manage. And Granddad is going to get me started with some stock."

A breeze blew over them and he looked beyond her. "It's going to be good out here. I just know it is. Let's go call Creighton before someone else gets to look at the place."

"I think you should take more time, but okay."

No one in her family would buy something the size of

this ranch within hours of looking at it. And she suspected if Jared could have taken her with him on the first viewing, he would have bid on it right then. It amazed her the man asked her opinion.

She rubbed her forehead again. How well would this news be received at the party tomorrow night?

Nine

The next day Jared said he would take Merry to Meg's and come later to the celebration because he would be delayed looking at records at the courthouse.

Faith dressed in a sleeveless deep blue dress with a straight skirt. An undercurrent of excitement ran through her, and she knew it wasn't the promotion or the party. She was looking forward to being with Jared tonight. Humming, she fastened her hair on her head and wore her diamond stud earrings.

When she arrived at the club, they were serving cocktails on the terrace and in the glassed sunroom. She accepted congratulations from her parents, her father beaming when he hugged her.

"I'm proud of you," he said.

"Thank you, Dad. Jared is going to be a little late. He had an appointment."

"Sure. Blake told me about the clients and accounts you've helped them acquire this year. That's good."

"Thank you."

"There's Blake now." When her father moved away, she saw Andy standing a few yards away watching her. He raised his glass of wine in a toast. "Congratulations," he said.

"Thank you."

"Where's the cowboy?"

"Jared had an appointment. He'll be along soon."

"Still the happy bride?"

"Yes, I am," she answered evenly, wondering how long her brother would feel antagonistic toward Jared.

She sensed someone watching her, and she turned and spotted Jared's dark head above the crowd. People moved and his gaze met hers.

"Here's Jared now. Excuse me, Andy." She walked away without looking back.

As Jared came into the room, surprise rippled in her. He was wearing a dark suit, dressed like other men in the room, yet he was far more handsome than any other man there. With his long hair, he still had that wild aura, and his Western boots that showed beneath the hem of his trousers set him apart from the others.

When she approached him, Jared's gaze slowly drifted down over her and back up to meet hers again, and she could see the approval in his dark eyes.

"You look great," he said when he reached her. "Good enough to haul out into the bushes and have my way with you."

"I'm about ready for you to do just that," she said, giving him a steady look. His dark brows arched, and she could see curiosity light his eyes.

"If that pleases you, then it more than suits me just fine, darlin'," he drawled in a husky voice. "It suits me a hell of a lot." He had always had that way of responding to her that made her feel sexy, all woman. "Let's stroll down the hall and look at the artwork."

Tempted, but remembering the party, she smiled and

shook her head. "You're not going to muss me up before the party starts. The only artwork to look at in the hall are pictures of past presidents of the club."

"Maybe they hung one of those Monets you like. Let's go see."

Unable to resist a few moments alone with him, she let him take her arm and lead her into the hall where they were alone, music growing soft in the background as glass doors closed behind them. She looked up at him, feeling her pulse skip at the desire she saw mirrored in his eyes.

"You're getting your way again," she remarked.

"You just told me what you wanted. We need some privacy."

"You're not going to make love to me here at the club!"

"We can always try the garden. In this heat we'd have it to ourselves."

She laughed, knowing he was teasing her, but the smoldering look in his eyes wasn't a tease, and her heart fluttered with anticipation. Clearly—and not in the throes of passion—she had told him what she wanted, and she couldn't imagine he would let her remark pass without acting on it.

He tightened his fingers on her arm, pulled her into an empty salon and closed the door.

"They might have plans for this room."

"So do I," he said, pulling her into his arms.

"You're wearing a suit I haven't seen."

"It's new. I got it so I would come a tad closer to fitting in with your family."

"Did you really?" she asked, wondering if her family made him feel like an outcast. "Well, I can tell you," she said in a throaty voice while she ran her hands over the lapels and then down to his thighs, "it is very sexy."

"I'll remember to wear it more often."

"Well, maybe not as sexy as those briefs you wear."

"So you noticed."

"I don't think I missed a thing. And I'm sure you didn't."

"I can remember everything you've worn in exact detail," he drawled, brushing light kisses along her temple and cheek and ear while his arm tightened around her waist.

"Remember, don't muss me. Dad will probably make some kind of toast and everyone will look at me and I don't want to look as if we've been—"

His open mouth covered hers, and she no longer cared about her hair or her dress. One touch was all it took and she was lost. When she felt his hand skim over her bottom and then pull her dress up to caress her thigh, she caught his wrist and stepped away. She twisted a lock of hair back in place on top of her head.

"We have to go back to the party. This is one night we'll be missed."

His eyes were the color of midnight and held flames that kept her pulse racing. "You go, darlin'. I'm in no shape to join everyone right now," he said in a husky voice. "I'll look at those club presidents' pictures and maybe cool down."

She left and in a few minutes he joined her. He took her arm and she walked around the room with him while he greeted her family and their guests until they separated, talking to different people. Later, she looked across the room to see him talking to a group that included two of her female friends from work, both sisters and her brother Keith. The women laughed at something he said, and even Keith seemed relaxed and was smiling. She tried to focus her attention on the cluster of people around her and listen to Blake talk about his day at the races.

Jared shifted, glancing across the room to meet his wife's gaze. Someone spoke to her and she looked away. His eyes ran over her again. She was a beautiful woman, and he wasn't going to keep waiting to make her his wife. She said she was ready, and the mere thought of her remark made him hot.

Wisdom said he should wait until their life together was more firmly established, but he was beginning to get lost in traffic and forget to do things he should because his thoughts were constantly on her. His nerves were stretched raw, and he couldn't remember having a good night's sleep since he had met her. He corrected himself wryly. He hadn't had a good night's sleep since he met Miss Merry. Between the two females in his life, his sleep was almost nil.

He excused himself from the group around him and moved to the bar, knowing he was the only person in the room drinking beer. But he had never acquired a taste for wine or champagne.

He saw the people in her group raise their glasses in a toast to her, and he was certain they were congratulating her on her promotion. He was glad for her and felt no threat from her job or her family, because the lady had been ready for a change from the first moment he met her. He wondered if she was beginning to like this new world he had pulled her into. A world of rodeos and travel and ranching and babies. And sex. He knew she liked that. And he knew that once they came together as man and wife, he would take her places she'd never dreamed possible. And if she should become pregnant, he hoped someday she would just flat leave her job and come home to be with their children.

"How's the cowboy?" a man asked behind him.

Jared turned to face Faith's stocky grandfather, who was the only man in the room without a suit and tie. He wore a blue sport shirt and slacks and shook hands amicably with him.

"Fine. Enjoying my wife's moment of glory."

"She ought to be home with the babies, but that will come in time." He tilted his head to study Jared. "It will, won't it? More than little Merry?"

"God willing."

"Where'd you get the beer?"

"Right here." Jared turned and asked the bartender for another beer.

"Thanks. This fizzy stuff has as much taste as creek water. Think you can keep riding those bulls when you get to be half my age?"

Jared smiled. "I hadn't really thought that far ahead, but I doubt it. I'm not sure I'll ride them more than another four or five years. It's good money, though."

"Yep, so I've read. Unless the bull gores you or something like that."

"I try to avoid getting in their way. By the way, I just bid on some land. I intend to start raising cattle as soon as the deal closes."

"Did Faith agree to this?"

"Yes, sir. The place is close to town so I can get back and forth."

"Or she can get back and forth. Well, good for you." He raised his beer. "Congratulations on your new ranch. I'm glad you came along. We need new blood in this family. I saw your finances. You're right good at that rodeoing, but that's hard work."

"So are a lot of other things," Jared remarked dryly.

"I haven't ridden a horse in forty years."

"Soon as we have our place, you come out and you can ride."

"Will you have anything tame enough? These old bones can't take much."

"Sir, I expect those old bones can take a hell of a lot, but, yes, I'll have something tame enough for you."

Grandpa Kolanko chuckled. "You're not scared of me, are you?"

"Why should I be?"

"I don't know, but I scared the wits out of the last fellow she dated. I think it was my money."

"Well, I don't want your money. They've announced dinner, sir. I'll go get my pretty wife."

"You do that."

Jared moved through the crowd and took Faith's arm. "Was Grandpa bothering you?"

"Hell, no. He's enjoyable."

She glanced up at Jared as if doubting what he said. "You're the first one to think so. He makes Andy and Keith nervous. He just irritates Dad because he'll say whatever comes to mind."

"That's plain old honesty and that's okay."

"I think my family is accustomed to a little finesse and subtlety."

"How's this for a little finesse and subtlety?" Jared asked softly, moving behind her in the crowd as they entered the dining room. Between them, hidden from the view of others, his hand drifted down over her bottom.

She turned her head slightly. "Someone is going to see you."

"Never. I have nimble fingers filled with finesse." His hand caressed her lightly across the bottom again, drifting down over her thigh.

"Congratulations, Faith," a tall, brown-haired man said.

"Thank you, Dan. Dan, this is my husband, Jared Whitewolf. Jared, Dan Haworth. Dan is Uncle Blake's and Dad's accountant."

"Glad to meet you," Jared said, shaking hands and then resting his hand on her shoulder.

"You almost got caught," she said when Haworth turned away.

"Like hell. Wait until we're seated and see what I can do beneath the table."

"You keep your hands to yourself until we get home!" she said, smiling and nodding at someone who called congratulations to her.

She went through dinner barely aware of anything except her handsome husband. His light caresses heaped more kindling on the fires already burning steadily in her.

As she cut into a thick, juicy steak, Jared leaned close to her.

"I've made an appointment to see Andy tomorrow."

Shocked, she lowered her fork. "Excuse me. I couldn't have heard correctly."

"Yes, you did. I want a will—"

"Why?" she asked, placing her fork on her plate and feeling chilled.

"I want him to look at the contract for the ranch and I need a will because of you and Merry. I want you listed as my beneficiary, and you and I should appoint a guardian for Merry if something happens to us. It's routine, Faith. Something I feel I should do as a father."

She thought of the dangers of bull riding and reached beneath the table to place her hand on his knee. "You think you can deal with Andy?"

"He has your interests at heart, so there shouldn't be a problem," he answered, his hand covering hers and lacing with her fingers to give her hand a squeeze. He released her and turned away as Meg said something to him.

Faith picked up her water to sip, realizing Jared was probably winning over her family, one by one. She wondered who would be the last one to lose his animosity toward her new husband—Andy or her dad.

During dessert she felt Jared's hand caress her knee. She was engaged in conversation with Porter, who sat on her left and she couldn't turn away. Slow, long, feathery strokes from Jared's fingers journeyed between her legs. She dabbed at her mouth with her napkin, placed it carefully over her lap and closed her fingers around his wrist. His arm stilled, but his fingers kept moving, just a slight rub, a faint pressure that made her body tense and desire ignite. She tried to focus on Porter, knowing she was losing the train of what he was saying.

Finally they stopped talking, and she turned to Jared.

"You're mighty free with your hands."

"Not as free as I'm going to be," he said softly.

The clinking of a spoon against a glass brought silence to the group, and her father stood up to propose a toast.

"To our new vice president. Best wishes in the coming year!"

Everyone murmured congratulations again while Faith stood. "I want to thank you, Mom and Dad, for the dinner tonight and thank Blake and my co-workers for all they've done." Faith turned to Porter and raised her glass.

"I would like to propose a toast to my co-worker and supervisor, Porter Gaston, Graphic Design's new Vice President of Accounts."

Everyone lifted their glasses in another toast and Porter acknowledged his thanks. Faith glanced at Jared who gazed at her with a sexy promise and faint hint of amusement in his dark eyes.

She sat down and conversation resumed while she turned to her husband. "Will you stop fondling me, because someone is going to notice."

"Notice what? That I like flirting with my wife? That isn't scandalous."

"What you're thinking is! And your hand is all over my legs."

"You think you know what's running through my mind?"

"I know how you're looking at me and what your hand is doing right now. Behave!" She had her knees pressed tightly together, but his fingers moved indolently back and forth where her legs touched together. Flames darted from each stroke of his hand.

"I'm barely touching you. What's the harm in a little playing around?"

"You make me want to slide right under the table and pull you down there with me, dinner or no dinner," she whispered, leaning close to his ear.

"Oh, darlin'. I had no idea—"

"The devil you didn't! Now I'm going to talk to Porter and you put your hand in your own lap."

"That's no fun!"

"Try a little circumspection until we get out of here."

"If that's what you want," he said with a sigh. "I'll bottle up all my natural inclinations brought about by that sexy little dress and the best-looking pair of legs I've ever seen."

"Thank you," she said, her pulse racing. He had stirred her to a white-hot flame of need. She wondered whether he realized the full effect he had on her. And how much did his flirting mean to him? She suspected it came as naturally to him as breathing.

She turned to Porter and didn't know whether she was really relieved or not that Jared kept his hands to himself.

Shortly after dinner, when they started to leave the party, Jared draped his arm across her shoulders as they headed toward the door. "We should tell Meg we're leaving and call Stan's mom to tell her we'll be there soon. We're the first to leave, you know," Faith said.

"I've already taken care of all that. I talked to Meg." He held the door open to the hallway and she went through, Jared falling into step beside her. "I asked Meg if she would mind keeping Merry all night."

"Why did you do that?"

"We've bid on the ranch. Even though it is night, I want to look at it one more time with you. By the time we drive there and back to town, it'll be late picking up Merry."

"Meg doesn't mind?"

"Not at all. You know your sister. She's like you. She could have a dozen kids and be happy as a clam."

"You don't know that about me," Faith replied, knowing he was right. She had missed Merry during their honeymoon, missed her when she went to work each day.

"Oh, yes, darlin'. On this point, I damn sure do. Tell me I'm wrong," he said, pausing at the front door to wait for her reply, blocking her path until she answered.

"You think you're so smart," she said primly, and he grinned, pushing open the door.

"Tell me about your new position—will you change

your office?'' he asked as they moved across the brightly lit parking lot.

"I move day after tomorrow, and you'll have to come see it.'' She talked while they drove out of the lot and headed southeast out of town. It was a perfect spring night with a full moon, cool breezes and twinkling stars overhead. She sat twisted in the seat where she could watch her husband. *Husband.* The word was still new and amazing to her. Mrs. Whitewolf. She didn't think of herself yet as Faith Whitewolf. Jared had fit in with her family tonight far better than she would have ever guessed. And he had found an ally in her maverick grandfather, who was too blunt and outspoken for the rest of the family.

They turned onto the dusty driveway, crossed the rickety bridge and soon passed the darkened ranch house. She looked at the moonlight splashing over it.

"Jared, in the moonlight the house looks lovely,'' she said, imagining how it would look remodeled.

"I know it does. It looks great in my imagination. It's a nice big house, and we can get it looking even better than the one on Peoria. And it has all that glass on the south side. It'll be filled with sunshine day and night.''

"Not night," she said, smiling.

He picked up her hand to brush a kiss across her knuckles. "You're the sunshine at night," he said softly.

Longing for him spilled through her. It had been a wonderful night with everyone showering her with good wishes, but it was the tall man beside her who had made the evening special.

"Jared, suppose Meg needs to get us for any reason?''

"Here's my cell phone. We'll hear it ring. Don't worry about Merry. Meg will have everything under control.''

As the pickup bounced over ruts and bumps, grass swishing against the vehicle, she looked at the rolling land. "How do you know where you're going? You're not even on a road.''

"I drove around when I was out here with Merry yesterday."

She wondered about his knack for the outdoors and animals. She would be hopelessly lost and never know where she had driven before, particularly if she hadn't stayed on a path.

They drove up a hill, and he parked near a tall oak with limbs spread like open arms. Jared climbed down, and when she stepped out of the pickup, silence enveloped her. He removed a blanket from the back and took her arm.

"You carry a blanket?" she asked, wondering about her husband's past.

"This is the blanket I took to the park for a picnic with Merry. Faith, there have been few women in my life since Merry's arrival."

"It wasn't any of my business, anyway," she replied, but she was glad of his answer.

"There are only two females in my life now, and one isn't even a year old yet," he said, spreading the blanket.

"Jared, what are you doing?"

"Enjoying you and our new home-to-be," he said, shedding his coat and tie. He unfastened the first buttons on his shirt, leaving a small vee of his chest showing. He strode back to her side. "Look around you."

He draped his arm across her shoulders, and she stood close enough beside him to feel the faint pressure of his hip against hers, the warmth of his body. Lush green land spread away from them in all directions, rolling, grassy and bright in the silvery moonlight, dark and shadowed where groves of trees stood. As breezes moved over the grass, it waved like a sea beneath the wind. In the distance, in a dip in the land, she could see the ranch house nestled near tall oaks. Near the house, moonlight shimmered on a stretch of the running stream.

"This is beautiful," she said, hearing only the sigh of the wind, wondering what her life would be like in the future.

"More beautiful than anything else in the world," he whispered in a husky voice, and turned her to him. It was then she realized he wasn't talking about the land, but about her. "You really are."

"No, I'm not," she whispered in return, "but I'm glad you think so." Her pulse raced, and when she saw the small bit of his chest revealed by his open shirt, she couldn't drag her attention away from it, remembering vividly how he looked bare chested.

"I want to go back and pick up a thread of conversation we had earlier tonight," he said.

"Do you really?" she asked while anticipation shook her. She was unable to stop staring at the small bit of his chest exposed by his unbuttoned shirt. In the moonlight his burnished skin looked darker than ever. She could detect his woodsy after-shave, a faint clean, soapy smell on his skin. She leaned forward, her tongue stroking that smooth bit of flesh, feeling his chest expand as he inhaled. "Because the last thing I want to do is talk."

Ten

Jared growled low in his throat, a deep masculine sound that made her feel wanted, sexy. She wanted him to love her. She wanted to love him, to please and touch and kiss him. This tough, wild man who was so strong and fearless had some voids in his life and she suspected he could stand some loving. And she was certain he was vulnerable where his heart was concerned.

He had kept his part of their marriage bargain. He had done everything he could to please her, including waiting as agreed to consummate the marriage, and allowing her to decorate the house on Peoria. He had bought a new suit to fit in with her family, consulted her on buying his ranch. Now she wanted to please him and she desperately wanted his loving.

It was time they tried to make the marriage real. Even though she had Merry, Faith was ready for another baby—Jared's baby.

He placed his hands on either side of her head and tilted

her face up to his while she carefully tried to work free the remaining buttons on his shirt.

Dark eyes bore into her as if searching for her feelings. "I want to make you mine in every way," he said in a husky voice that was tight with emotion. Was she really as vital to him as he said?

His fingers slid over her head, shaking free the pins, causing her hair to tumble down over her shoulders. "We took a vow to have and to hold. I want you to want that with all your being. Including everything it implies."

Her breathing jammed, her heart raced and her body trembled from the searching of his dark eyes. He lowered his head, laying siege to her mouth, giving to her, stirring up a storm that roared around them.

Caught in the vortex of emotion he created, she stood on tiptoe, winding her arms around his neck. Her fingers tangled with the leather tied around his hair and it fell free. She felt the coarse strands slide over her bare arms, knew she held and kissed a man so different from herself. A cowboy whose wild streak she loved and needed even though it took her breath and scared her senseless.

She shoved his shirt off his shoulders, letting her fingers travel over the bulge of powerful muscles, feeling the strength in the arm tightly banded around her waist. His kisses had unleashed a tidal wave of desire that rushed over her.

She ached low in her body, a hollow craving that only he could fill. She was not a virgin, yet no man really existed before Jared. No man had ever driven her to the depths of need like he did. No man had ever stirred such a storm of passion or treated her as if she was the sexiest woman on earth.

"I need you," Jared said, his mouth covering hers, his tongue stroking hers, moving in a rhythm that created a gush of heat that centered between her legs.

"Jared, I don't have much experience—"

"Darlin', that's one thing we don't have to worry about.

The yesterdays are gone. It's us and now," he whispered, and she accepted what he said as passion overwhelmed her.

His hands slid slowly over her, down her sides, over her hips and thighs and then around, moving languorously to the top of her dress. He tugged down the zipper, and the air was cool across her back and shoulders when he pushed the dress away. As it fell to the grass in a heap, he leaned back. His hands stilled while he took in the sight of her.

"You're beautiful," he said in a voice that sounded full of awe. Watching her, he slid his fingers slowly up her rib cage, moving to her breastbone. He flicked the catch to her bra and pushed it away. He palmed her breasts, and her body tensed, hot and eager. While he held her lightly, he leaned down. His tongue stroked around the nipple, making her groan and cling to him, her need heightening to a frenzy. Her breasts tightened, ached for his mouth, and then he took her nipple in his mouth, his tongue stroking in a sweet torment, his teeth biting just enough to send little shocks streaking in her.

Jared shook, fighting for control. Since that first afternoon he had wanted her in his arms, bare, open to him. He wanted her softness surrounding him, her body beneath his, and he felt he had waited aeons for this night.

"I want you, Faith. I want us to love out here on our land where we'll have our family. Our home and our hearts will be here," he said, the words a husky rasp, and he had no idea whether she heard him or not. Then she turned her head, trailing kisses on his throat.

"Who's planning now?" she whispered. Her tongue flicked over his ear and tension wound tighter in him. "I thought you never planned ahead," she whispered with her eyes closed, her hands stroking him. She opened her eyes to look at him. "You're planning your life. And mine."

"Life's a gamble," he said, "but love is something you can plan on. It's rock solid."

His answer was sharp, but the part about love shook her.

How could he feel so sure about something he didn't know? "You can't know yet what we'll have together."

"I know what I feel and what I want," he answered in a husky rasp.

She drew a deep breath, and he wondered whether she believed him or not. He bent to kiss her breast, caressing the other breast, his thumb rolling over her nipple while his tongue stroked a taut peak. Her hands fluttered over his chest and back, sliding lower and caressing him, exploring each plane and angle as if she was as desperate to know his body as he was to know hers. Her fingers were a raging torment that threatened his control.

He wanted a place and a moment in time she wouldn't forget. *He* would never forget, but he was head over heels, heart and soul in love with the woman and she couldn't see it and wouldn't believe him if he told her.

He picked her up, set her on her feet on the blanket, and then he stepped back again to look at her while he yanked off first one of his boots and then the other.

As he straightened, her wide green eyes met his gaze. Moonlight splashed over her features, and while she might not think love was possible yet and might not be in love with him, she wanted him. Desire smoldered in her eyes like a burning fire. She still wore flimsy lace panties and her thigh-high hose. He ran his finger along the top of one of her stockings, feeling her firm satin-smooth skin.

"If I had known there was some bare leg up higher—"

"It's a good thing you didn't know," she interrupted, stroking his chest, her fingers drifting down to his waist. She reached out to unfasten his trousers. Her slender fingers were deft, sure. When his pants fell, he stepped out of them.

Faith inhaled, her body steaming. His manhood was thick, already thrusting out of the low-cut briefs. She hooked her fingers in the elastic band and pushed them away, drawing them down his strong legs and feeling the rough texture of short hairs on his legs scrape against her palms.

She stayed on her knees to curl her fingers around his hard shaft as she leaned forward to kiss him. He gasped, his fingers tangling roughly in her hair, and then he hauled her to her feet to kiss her. While he kissed her, the last flimsy bits of her clothing flew. Urgency made his hands shake and sent tremors of desire racing in her.

He picked her up, her body bare and warm against his naked body. Holding her close, he knelt on the blanket, still kissing her when he lowered her on it. Then he moved down her body to caress the slight arch of her foot. Her bones felt delicate, so special to him. "Every inch of you is beautiful to me."

Faith stared at him, his words spinning in her mind. This strong cowboy followed his impulses. What havoc would he wreak in her life? And what pleasure? Her need for him was crushing, all-consuming. She watched him steadily as he leaned down to trail his tongue from her foot to the inside of her knee while his dark eyes were on her. She rested on her elbows, watching him, wanting to reach for him, tingling from every stroke of his hands and mouth. As he looked at her, his dark eyes drew her into midnight depths where reason and plans vanished.

"I want you, Faith," he whispered.

She reached for him. Her hand cupped the back of his neck and she sat up, pulling him forward to kiss him, trailing her tongue across his lips and then sliding her tongue into his mouth. He leaned over her to kiss her long and hard. When he moved away, he trailed kisses down her throat, to her breast. He lowered her to the blanket as his foray dipped lower across her belly, his tongue a flash of hot fire. Then he spread her legs and trailed kisses between her thighs, his tongue stroking, circling, showering wet hot kisses on the center of her warmth.

She cried out, arching, her thighs spread, ready for him, her hands clutching his shoulders. He shifted, his hand going where his mouth had been on the sweet, hot bud. He stroked and rubbed, building a pressure in her while she clung to him, her hips moving. With each stroke he could feel the tightening in her body.

"Jared, please, I want you," she whispered.

He wasn't sure he could last another ten seconds, but he damned well was going to try to hold back. He was going to make her remember this night, and he wanted to forge a bond between them that would last through the days to come. He was claiming his woman with his hands and his mouth, taking possession of her body, hoping it ran deeper and he was uniting with her soul.

Faith cried out, tumbling over a brink only to want him more than ever. She gripped his arms, pulling him to her. "Jared, I need you and want you. I ache—"

He swooped down, his mouth capturing hers as if he could take her words and keep them forever. He straightened and moved between her legs and then reached for his pants to remove a packet. He was poised over her, virile, his manhood hard and ready.

She took his hand. "No. You know I want a baby."

"You're the one who always says not to rush into something."

"Maybe I'm learning from you," she answered breathlessly. "Are you going to talk all night?"

He tossed aside the packet and lowered his body. She felt the velvet tip of his manhood touch her and she arched her hips, a hot shimmer of excitement making her quiver. She slid her long legs around him, her hands running down over his lean body, down over his firm buttocks as she caressed him and tugged him closer.

He thrust into her. She was incredibly tight and he paused, sweat pouring off him while he tried to control his urges. "Darlin', I'm going to hurt you."

"Never!" she gasped, her legs tightening around him while her fingers dug into his buttocks and he was lost. He thrust into her, hearing her cry.

"Ahh, Jared, how I've wanted you!" she whispered, moving wildly beneath him, her head thrashing, and he knew he wasn't hurting her. Far from it. Then thought stopped as he moved with her, kissing her, trying to be joined with her as much as humanly possible.

Tension pounded him, building until he knew he wasn't going to last any longer. Dimly he heard her cry, felt her arch higher beneath him, felt wild spasms rock her. She was fire and passion, burning him to cinders.

"Faith, love!" he ground out the words, thrusting deep within her, wishing he could hold her forever. She clung to him, their bodies locked together. Rapture ripped him apart; his fire and substance spilled into her. She was his woman now and forever.

Faith felt as if she were settling back to earth from a ride across the sky on a shooting star. Only Jared had been no shooting star, but a flesh-and-blood man whose lovemaking was wild and passionate and breathtaking. She stroked his back, still wanting him, aware of the kisses he showered over her temple, cheek and throat.

Winding her fingers in his dark hair, she was amazed at the depth of her reaction to him, astounded at the abandon she had shown. How deep did her feelings for him run? Was she falling in love with this wild man she had married? She stroked him, feeling a breeze cool her damp shoulders, the rest of her body bearing his weight, their legs tangled together.

"I never, ever would have believed that one night I would make love to a man on a blanket out in the woods under a starry sky. You're a wild man, Jared Whitewolf."

"And you're a fine, wild woman. And it's pretty damned nice to make love under the stars, don't you think?"

"Yes, it is," she answered shyly, remembering how wantonly she had loved and responded to him. And it amazed her now to lie naked in his arms and feel the wind blow over their sated bodies. Never in her life had she dreamed of doing such a thing. He shifted beside her and pulled her close in the circle of his arms.

"Darlin', you finished me off." He propped his head on

his hand to look down at her and he smiled. "And it was a damned good finishing, too."

She traced the line of his jaw, surprised by the night, still astounded to be married to such a man.

"You're a rash, impulsive man." She grew silent while his hand trailed over her, gentle strokes that made her feel cherished. Her thoughts drifted to the part of his life that worried her. "But if I fall in love with you, I don't think I can take your bull riding. How long do you plan to keep on doing it?"

"Your grandfather just asked me that a few hours ago. I haven't planned what I'll do. Ride until I don't want to ride, I guess."

Moonlight splashed over her, and Jared looked at his bride's curvaceous, beautiful body that lay bare to his view. Soft, wondrous—she was all he had hoped for and much more. He felt boneless, unable to stand or move more than his hand as it slightly stroked her. Her skin was silky smooth. Her golden cascade of hair was disheveled, fanned behind her head and on her milky shoulders. Her skin was lovely, pale next to his. Pink and white and golden. His hand strayed to a full breast and he traced her aureole.

"Jared." Her voice was languid.

He lay down beside her and pulled her close as they lay on their sides, facing each other.

"This is perfect," he said, his bass voice a deep rumble.

"It's perfect tonight. I don't want to sleep out here on this hill every night."

"We'll sleep in our bed in the big bedroom in the house, but I wanted this tonight. I feel part of this place, and now a part of you."

Faith's pulse drummed at his words, but she found it difficult to believe him. He was rash, impetuous, impulsive—he had never settled in his life. Would he really settle now? Another inkling of worry intruded.

"Jared, have you ever done anything besides rodeo riding?"

He chuckled, a deep-throated sound that came up from the depths of his chest. "'Course I have, darlin'. I've hired on ranches, done bronc busting, worked for a vet once. I've worked for a blacksmith and I can shoe horses. I worked for an electrician for a time. I've cooked, washed dishes, driven race cars."

"What's the longest you've ever lived in any one place?"

"I didn't keep count, so I don't have any idea."

"Surely you would know if you'd spent years in a place," she said, aware he nudged her legs apart with his and twined his leg high between hers. His body was heated, slightly damp. His breathing had returned to normal as had hers, and he was still trailing his fingers over her. From her waist over the curve of her hip, then along her thigh. She drew a deep breath. How could he stir desire in her so easily?

"Darlin', I've never in my life spent years in any one place. Our mother moved all over the U.S., and after I ran away, I traveled across country and into Mexico and up into Canada. While you, luscious woman," he said, nuzzling her neck, "aside from college, have probably lived right here."

Faith felt his shaft, hard against her thigh, and knew he was aroused again. Her pulse jumped as his casual strokes changed to caresses that started a blaze. She shifted, feeling a wrench of desire. Her hands moved over his chest while he showered her with kisses.

Jared wanted her again. He suspected the next thousand years wouldn't be enough to satisfy him. She was lush, naked, too tempting. And he was remembering the past hour and their torrid lovemaking. Erotic images taunted him. He shifted, lying on his back, and pulled her on top of him to play with her breasts before raising his head to take a nipple in his mouth.

He wanted her more now than he had wanted her before. He knew he might have sealed his own fate. If she got pregnant from their lovemaking, she would have the baby she'd always wanted. But if their marriage didn't work out, where would that leave Merry and him? He knew his fear was premature—and perhaps even paranoid—but he couldn't imagine life without Faith in it.

And he didn't want to stop. The marriage was consummated and there was no turning back now. He stroked her back, his hand sliding around over her stomach, down to the tangle of soft curls, searching, finding the ready bud, teasing and hearing her cry out as her fingers tightened on his shoulders.

"Here's the best kind of ride, darlin'," he whispered. He lifted her hips, settling her on his hard shaft while a storm of passion broke over them.

Faith moved with abandon, shocks of pleasure raking her while his hands played with her and moonlight spilled over their bodies. She felt wild, free, amazed at her zest for lovemaking.

Rapture burst as she felt his deep thrust, his hands clenching her hips. And then she felt as if she melted into a boneless puddle on top of him. His arms, sure and strong, enveloped her, and he kissed her damp temple, murmuring endearments that she barely heard through her still-thundering pulse.

They slept in each other's arms. Then Faith woke to his caresses and loving again. And they slept and loved again, each time their need and passion seeming stronger than the time before. As the first faint pink tinged the sky and stars faded from sight in the eastern sky, she lay exhausted in his arms.

"Jared, it's morning. We're stark naked out here."

"So who's going to see us?" he drawled, amusement lacing his voice.

"I have to be at work in a couple of hours! I don't even know what time it is!"

He rolled over to look at her and smiled, brushing a kiss across her lips. "So I'll get you to work maybe just a little late, but they'll understand. Tell them we were making out all night—''

"I'll do no such thing!" she exclaimed, and saw the twinkle in his eyes. She slapped her palm against his shoulder. "Devil!"

"Sexy lady. I'll bet you haven't been late to work ever."

"Maybe once or twice—and the last time was on my lunch break when I met you. See what you do to my life?" she said, standing up. She blushed, waving her hands. "Where are my clothes?"

"You look damned good this way," he said in a husky voice, standing, his shaft hard and ready.

"I have to go to work."

"Do you really?" he asked, stepping close to kiss her throat. His hand stroked her breast, his thumb playing over her nipple and she moaned.

"Jared, I will be so *late*—"

"It'll be worth it," he whispered.

Within minutes, she decided it was.

Eleven

Faith leaned forward, her fists knotted as she stared through the glass down at the arena and then looked at the television screen in the private box. They were at a Texas rodeo, and she sat with Jared's friends and their wives in a plush box in a fancy arena. The television camera took her right down into the chute with Jared and she watched him secure his hand to the broad back of the Brahman bull.

The buzzer sounded, and she shifted her gaze from the television to the window. Everyone around her ceased to exist. Her entire focus was on Jared as the bull leaped in the air and twisted in a corkscrew turn. She closed her eyes, unable to watch, finding each rodeo more devastating than the last. It was late July now, and she had been watching him compete since that first week she had met him in April. And her fear had only grown worse with each competition.

Someone nearby gasped and fingers clamped on her arm.

"Faith, he's all right," a deep voice said. "He'll be okay," Bud Tarkington, one of Jared's friends, repeated.

Faith opened her eyes and saw Jared dangling from the bull as it made another violent leap, kicking the air and twisting as if trying to shake free of the cowboy flopping against its broad side.

Jared fell, a hoof coming down on him. Then the clowns dashed in, waving bandannas at the bull. Jared got up and walked over to pick up his hat. He scooped it up stiffly, staggered a step and then righted himself.

She fled from the box. She didn't know whether she'd said anything to the others or not. She couldn't stand his riding and now he was hurt. If he hadn't walked out of the arena on his own, she would have fainted right there in the box.

She rushed through the cavernous halls and down concrete steps, holding the cold iron railing as she dashed back to where the pens and animals and riders were.

She found Jared sitting on a cask while a paramedic taped his ribs. He looked up, grinned, and then his smile faded. "Thanks, Gene."

"Sit still while I fasten this. You need to go to a hospital and get an X ray to make sure you don't have a punctured lung. Don't lift anything heavy. And stay off the bulls."

"Yeah, right. Thanks. This is my wife, Faith Whitewolf. Faith, this is Gene Cole."

She nodded, unable to say anything.

"Glad to meet you, ma'am. You can drive him to the hospital."

As she nodded, the paramedic snapped shut a bag and then moved away. Jared stood, going to her. "Look, I'm okay."

"I'm not," she said stiffly. "Jared, I couldn't stand seeing you hurt."

"I'll mend."

"This time! Suppose it had been your neck? I can't take your riding. You're a father now. Merry needs you. She's already lost her mother and a daddy who loved her."

"Faith, I just cracked some ribs."

She looked away as his hands settled on her shoulders. "I've never done anything very physical," she said. "I barely can swim. I don't ski. I'm not accustomed to that kind of life and I just can't cope with it." She looked into his eyes. "Will you stop bull riding?"

Jared gazed into green eyes filled with concern and fear and he knew he couldn't push aside her worries as nothing. "Darlin', at the rate I'm going, I'll qualify for the National Finals. That's a helluva lot of money that we need. I've never been badly hurt. A few broken bones is all."

"You could get killed and you know it."

"I told you, you run the same risk on the freeway."

"Don't be ridiculous! Jared, give it up, please," she said, feeling desperate. His determination to keep competing reminded her of the chasm between their feelings. She was deeply in love with this wild cowboy, while he didn't love her enough to give up his reckless ways.

He slid his arm around her and turned her to walk with him. "Let's go pick up Merry from your folks' house and go home."

"We're going straight to the hospital."

"If that pleases you, then it suits me just fine, darlin'," he drawled.

She walked with him through the arena and out into a warm night. "I'll drive," she said, climbing behind the wheel.

They rode in silence to the hospital, where he disappeared while she took care of the admitting details and then sat, waiting. She looked at the pale green walls, the fluorescent lights overhead, the tall vending machines that held snacks and drinks, but her thoughts were elsewhere, racing over the night. When she saw Jared get hurt, she hurt. And she could barely breathe. And she knew now that she was deeply in love with him.

The realization was startling. At the same time, it seemed as if she had loved him a long, long time. He was everything she needed. He filled the voids in her life. He was her soul mate. Because in many ways they were alike. They loved Merry with a deep intensity. And she loved the ranch and could see the beauty he saw. And maybe she needed his recklessness to balance her caution.

I love him. How long had she loved him without acknowledging it? How long was she going to wait before she told him?

She thought back to that first night when he had made love to her beneath the starry sky, and she knew she had loved him then. That was not just lust. It had gone far deeper with her and she knew it did with him. She had given him her body that night, and her heart.

She gazed down the empty hospital corridor, wanting Jared to come striding down it, wanting to throw herself into his arms and tell him.

She loved him, this tall, lean cowboy who was a continual surprise and delight in her life. This sexy lover, reliable father, true companion. And because she loved him, she couldn't live with his bull riding.

She couldn't help but notice the irony. Had she realized she loved him at the moment she was going to have to leave him?

She heard the jingle of spurs and the scrape of boots as Jared came back down the hall, and her pulse jumped. He held out his hands and grinned. "Lungs fine. Ribs will be okay soon. Let's go home."

They went through the doors and into the night. As they reached the pickup, she turned to him, taking his arm. "Jared."

He looked down at her and his brows arched quizzically.

"I know it's not the most romantic spot—we should be in a better place than a parking lot. But I want to tell you now. I love you."

Jared's heart thudded until he thought it would burst in his chest. He held her, trying not to crush her to him too tightly, ignoring the pain in his ribs from holding her so close. Tears stung his eyes and a lump filled his throat while joy consumed him. "Ah, my darlin'. I've waited since that first afternoon to hear those words. Ah, Faith, how I love you. My darlin' Faith."

His words thrilled her, and her pulse jumped. Yet wisdom nagged with the worry that plagued her—how deep did his love run? Enough to give up his bull riding? Would he put her and Merry first, before the wild thrills he also loved?

She clung to him, kissing him, knowing problems that might be insurmountable loomed, but for this moment, they loved each other. She loved him, and now he knew she did. And he loved her in return.

She had no idea how long they stood in the parking lot kissing, but someone drove past and honked and she realized where they were. She pushed against his chest. "We're creating a scene. We should go."

"Yes, ma'am. Let's go home."

She unlocked the pickup door and worries came tumbling back. As Jared gingerly climbed into the passenger seat, she thought about tomorrow night's rodeo.

When she drove out of the hospital parking lot, she glanced at him and saw him turned in the seat, studying her quietly.

"Faith, I stand to win too much to quit. And I'm not hurt that bad."

Hurt stabbed her heart. The reminder of the rodeo made vivid pictures of his being thrown from the bull dance in her mind. Her brief joy vanished and was replaced by concern. "You're going to ride again tomorrow night, aren't you? Even with your ribs taped."

"I haven't decided."

His words chilled her because he hadn't ruled out competing. And she knew he was going to. She couldn't stand watching him ride, risking everything, and she wasn't going to again.

"You have a baby to think about, if you're not going to worry about my feelings."

"Darlin', I worry about your feelings a hell of a lot. I just know the dangers better than you do, and you've blown them all out of proportion in your mind."

"I have money you can use for the ranch."

"You save your money. You might need it sometime," he answered.

"Jared, I can't take your bull riding. I can't sit by and watch you get hurt. I can't live with that. You have to decide—bull riding or our marriage."

He reached over to brush her cheek with his fingertips. "Darlin', you know what's most important to me. And tonight was a bad night. Give it a little time."

She wondered whether he realized how deep her feelings went—both her love for him and her dreadful worry for his safety.

"I meant what I said."

"I know you do right now, darlin', but my world is new to you," he answered gently.

She drove in silence, her thoughts whirring, while her jangled nerves tried to calm.

He'd been spending every day at the ranch and had a crew working on the house. They would soon be able to move into it, and she suspected that he wanted to—no matter their original agreement. His grandfather had delivered a truckload of cattle, and Jared had bought two cutting horses and a gentle mare for her.

And the time was fast approaching when he wouldn't be able to care for Merry during the day. Meg was keeping her now at least one day a week, and Faith's mother was also keeping her a day. Jared said he would write an ad for a nanny. The drive to the ranch was an hour—not an impossible commute—and she knew that the time would come when he would want her to be the one to commute because he would need to get up at dawn to go to work.

Now instead of a man of substance, he was a man deeply in debt. It was going to take long hours and hard work to make the ranch pay, and the first years would be critical.

And he could ease up his financial crunch with his rodeo winnings, but what good would that do if he were permanently injured or killed?

When they reached her parents' house, they picked up Merry, who was asleep, and drove to their house on Peoria.

Faith tucked Merry into bed, running her fingers over the child's silky curls. She bent down to kiss her soft cheek.

She went to the kitchen to open a can of pop. Moments later Jared came in with a towel wrapped around his waist. His hair was damp from his shower and she drew a swift breath, her pulse jumping at the sight of his smooth bronze skin and muscled chest above the stark white bandaging.

"Don't start sweet-talking me," she said forcefully. "Even with broken ribs and the doctor telling you not to, you're going to ride tomorrow night, aren't you?"

"If I don't hurt any worse than right now—yes. I want to ride. Faith, I can't give this up. And there's no reason to. You're scared because it's not familiar to you."

"I'm scared because I'm not a daredevil who doesn't show an ounce of caution."

He crossed the room to the refrigerator to get a can of beer and popped the top. He took a long drink, set the can on the table and crossed the room to face her.

Every step closer to her he took, her pulse revved up several notches. "Don't try to change the subject," she whispered as his arm slid around her waist.

"Darlin', all I can think about is that you said you love me." He leaned down, his mouth claiming her, destroying her arguments and burning her fear and anger to cinders.

Two hours later she lay in the curve of his arm, his long leg between her legs while he slept, and she stared into the darkness. She couldn't live in a constant state of fear, and she knew they were on a collision course about a lot of other things in their married life. It was time to get a nanny for Merry. She knew Jared wanted to move to the ranch. She thought about the long commute to work and dreaded it, yet that might be the only solution. She could see them working out everything except the real obstacle in their marriage: his bull riding. He wasn't going to give it up and she couldn't live with it.

Tears stung her eyes and she wiped at them, realizing she might have rushed into a terrible mistake. In the most basic way they weren't suited. They'd been married only three months, but compatibility wasn't coming with time.

She turned her head. Moonlight spilled across the big bed and she looked at her handsome husband, whose dark hair covered half his face and cheek. He looked as wild and masculine asleep as he did awake. Maybe more with his long hair falling across his face. And she loved him deeply and had been in love with him for a long time now.

She reached out, running her finger along his firm jaw, feeling tiny bristles. Her fingers moved lightly across his chest and desire stirred. Their lovemaking was fantastic, exciting. If only he wasn't so reckless about his rodeo riding!

She lay back in the darkness, knowing a few more caresses and he would wake and they would love again. She ran her hand across her forehead, wondering what she should do.

On Saturday night she kissed him goodbye at the door while she held Merry in her arms. In spite of taped ribs, he was going to ride in the rodeo. This time she wasn't going to watch.

"I'll be home by half past eleven. We can go out with the crowd if you want. We could take Merry along. She's no trouble."

Faith shook her head, feeling as if she was kissing him goodbye for longer than just tonight. "No. I want to stay home."

His dark eyes studied her, and she gazed back steadfastly, feeling a clash of wills between them. Then he slipped his hat on his head and brushed a fleeting kiss across her lips. "Take care." With a jingle of spurs and a scrape of his boot heels on the concrete, he strode across the drive and climbed into his pickup to drive away.

She closed and locked the door and hugged Merry, feeling tears sting her eyes as she prayed that he would be safe. He had a rodeo the next weekend in Phoenix and then another one in San Diego the following weekend. They had planned the trip together, and she'd intended to take Merry along, but that morning she'd canceled her flight. She and Merry would not go with him.

Merry wriggled and Faith carried her to the family room to set her on a blanket on the floor. She crossed her legs and sat down to play with Merry, but all the while her stormy thoughts were on Jared.

She was coming out of the shower after eleven when the phone rang. She heard Bud Tarkington's voice on the line and her heart lurched.

"Faith, Jared's okay, but he wanted me to call you to tell you he'll be late getting home."

She relaxed slightly, wondering if he had gone partying after the rodeo with the others, feeling a strange rift that he would go without her.

"Fine," she answered evenly.

"He had a little accident tonight."

"What happened? Where are you?" Her fears rushed back, and she gripped the receiver tightly.

"We're at the hospital and he's giving 'em hell now to let him go. A bull kicked him and he has a slight concussion. If he doesn't get out of here soon, he said to tell you he'll call you. They're trying to talk him into staying for observation."

"Bud, try to talk him into staying. I can be there in less than half an hour."

"No need," Bud answered casually. "He'll probably be released by then. He just wanted you to know where he was so you wouldn't worry."

"Thanks," she said, replacing the receiver when Bud said goodbye.

A *concussion*. The doctors wanted him in the hospital tonight, but she knew he would talk them into releasing him. She just couldn't cope with his reckless life-style. He was too wild, too willing to take huge risks.

Didn't he love his wife and child enough to take care of himself? Apparently his behavior spoke for itself where she was concerned.

She paced the floor until he came home, rehearsing a dozen speeches and ultimatums that all flew right out of her mind when she saw him. He had a bandage across his temple and he looked full of vitality, as if he hadn't received a scratch.

She flew into his arms to kiss him, all thoughts of discussion gone. His mouth met hers, and his strong arms reassured her that he was very much all right.

Jared held her and kissed her hard, wanting her and hating that she hadn't gone with him tonight even though he had been thankful she wasn't there to see him get hurt. From the moment he regained consciousness in the ambulance and his fuzzy thoughts cleared, he worried about facing her.

When he had stepped through the back door, his worries evaporated. Her pale face and green eyes showed only concern. Without a word of dissension, she had raced across the room into his arms.

Surprise and pleasure engulfed him and he bent his head to kiss her hungrily. He probably wouldn't have been thrown from the bull if he had been concentrating better. He was still intoxicated by her declaration of love.

Her hands fluttered over him as if she had to reassure herself that he was actually in her arms, and his heart pounded with joy. His arousal was swift and hard, a hungry need for her, his urgency matching hers. He tugged her T-shirt over her head, tossing aside the flimsy bra as he bent to take her nipple in his mouth. He wanted her and he wanted to give to her because she had bestowed the biggest gift of all on him when she said she loved him.

As he kissed her and flicked his tongue over the taut peak, his fingers deftly unfastened the buttons of her cutoffs and he shoved them away.

"I was so worried," she whispered. "I don't want to hurt your ribs—"

"You can't," he said, yanking off his own shirt. Driven to possess her, to feel her softness, he flung aside clothing. His pulse pounded, drowning out sounds. His hands roamed over her. He wanted to thrust himself into her dark warmth that bound them completely. He went down on his knees, his tongue tracing a fiery pattern as she parted her legs and moaned.

Urgency was as great in her as it was in him. Jared pulled her down, and as Faith stretched on the kitchen floor, he moved between her legs.

"Jared, your ribs—"

His mouth stopped conversation. Faith's heart drummed and her hands ran across his strong shoulders. He was home, safe, loving her, and at the moment that was all that mattered. His shaft slid into her warmth and Faith gasped with pleasure, wrapping her legs around him while they both moved in a frenzy of passion. Release burst in her, a white-hot, all-consuming pleasure. "I love you," she whispered.

"My darlin'," he gasped. "My love!"

Spasms of pleasure racked his body and she held him, still moving with him, lifted up and carried to another brink, feeling the pressure build and then burst in another release while she cried his name. His arms tightened around her and his weight settled on her as they slowed.

"Ah, love." He showered kisses on her. "I missed you being there tonight."

"You should be in the hospital."

"And miss this? Not on your nelly, darlin'!"

She closed her eyes and held him as he trailed kisses

over her temple and stroked her. He was here and safe in her arms and that was what was important for now. Tomorrow she would face the future, but this hour, she wasn't going to think about anything but his kisses and lovemaking.

Finally, after lying sated in each other's arms, he rolled over and then stood. When she rose beside him, she started to pick up her clothes. Instead, he lifted her into his arms.

"Jared, you'll hurt yourself."

"Stop worrying. I'm not going to do anything I shouldn't."

"Oh, not much, you aren't. You've been doing things you shouldn't since I met you," she accused, and he gave her a lopsided grin.

"Like making love on the kitchen floor," he said.

"We should get our clothes."

"No one is here to see them. Merry won't care or know." He felt a splash of tears on his chest. "Hey, darlin'."

In the bedroom he set her on her feet. He bent down to tilt her face up, his thumbs wiping away the tears as he brushed her face with his lips, trailing kisses to her ear. "I'm here and I'm just fine."

"They wanted you in the hospital for observation. Aren't you supposed to be awakened periodically through the night?"

"Yep. And we can do that right here at home."

"I'm setting your alarm and mine, so I'll be sure to wake up," she said firmly, moving to first one bedside table and then the other.

Jared caught her around the waist as she finished setting the second clock.

"I'll be sure to get you up."

"I know you will, darlin'. In the meantime, come here," he drawled.

He kissed her and she clung to his neck and kissed him

back until he stretched out on the bed and pulled her into his arms.

In minutes, as Jared stroked her, he felt her relax, and soon he could feel her deep, even breathing.

As she slept, he held her in his arms. He knew he should be in the hospital for observation, but he wanted to be home with Faith, and he was thankful they had released him. And he had heard her whisper of love in the throes of passion.

He stroked hair away from her nape. Her body had cooled and she drew steady breaths. He didn't know whether she was exhausted and slept because of their passion or because of the release of tension over her fears about his safety. Or a combination of both. Usually he was the one asleep first. Or so she told him. He stroked her throat, her bare shoulder, knowing he could push the sheet away and start the fires all over again.

He loved her more than ever. He had thought if they consummated their marriage, he would get his sanity back and stop thinking about her every waking minute. Instead, it was worse than ever. He was wildly, head-over-heels in love, and her feelings ran deeper than he'd realized. There was no mistaking the way she had thrown herself into his arms, showering kisses on him, tearing at his clothes with an urgency that went beyond any sheer physical need.

His thoughts shifted to bull riding. He couldn't give it up. He was piling up winnings, earning money that would relieve some of the debt he had taken them into. And he still didn't feel it was that dangerous. People ran risks every day. He did on the ranch; Faith did on her way to and from work.

He shifted, touching the bandage lightly. His head pounded as if someone were swinging a sledgehammer into it. But a month from now it wouldn't matter. He could not give up his riding, and he was banking on her growing love to get them through this.

Over the next four days, they argued over their future without coming to any conclusion. As he packed to leave for Phoenix, Faith watched him while Merry babbled and crawled on the floor, playing with plastic blocks.

"Jared." Faith took a deep breath, wondering whether she would regret what she was going to say. "We've discussed this before. If you go to Phoenix and San Diego and ride in the rodeos, I won't be here when you come back."

He halted, his eyes narrowing as he focused on her. He dropped his carry-on over a chair and crossed the room to place his hands on her hips. "Faith, that's absurd. We're going to have a lot of money from this. It's like my asking you to give up your job."

"I don't think it's the same at all," she replied, knowing that if he kept his distance, she would have the strength to speak from her heart. Tears stung her eyes. She was losing him. She was losing Merry. And she loved them both with all her heart. So much that she couldn't bear the risks that Jared took with his life—with his family's livelihood.

He gazed at her solemnly. "Darlin', we all gotta do what we gotta do," he said quietly, and her heart squeezed painfully. She had always wondered if he was easygoing about everything he encountered in life, but she saw now that when he felt strongly about something, he dug in his heels and wouldn't yield an inch.

"Just give up the bull riding, that's all I ask. Go ahead and continue the saddle bronc riding."

"Bull riding is what I do best. It's all I've ever been good at," he said quietly. "I'd like to please you. Damn well I'd like to, but this is income we need, and it's something I can do to support this family, and it doesn't scare me. I have to do this, Faith."

"You want the bull riding more than our marriage?"

"Hell, no. I'm hoping you'll come around to my side of it."

"I'm not going to. I can't. The risks you take are just too great. I haven't liked this from the start, and it's only gotten worse with each rodeo. Jared, I can't bear it when you get hurt.''

"For a woman ready to walk out, you care a damn lot about my welfare,'' he remarked. "Did you mean what you said about love?''

"Yes,'' she answered in a forlorn whisper. "But did you?''

"Damn right.'' He stepped forward, tightened his arm, and his mouth covered hers. His tongue slid deep into her mouth, stroking hers, hot, demanding, reminding her of every intimacy they had shared.

She could no more resist responding than she could resist breathing. Winding her arms around his neck, she kissed him passionately in return, trying to hold him with kisses, trying to make him see that they had something fine and special between them that he was destroying.

His hand tangled in her hair and his other hand slid down, his palm caressing her bottom as he pulled her tightly against him. His arousal pressed against her and she trembled, wanting him, wanting to change his mind, to hold him. Wanting him to love her enough to give up bull riding.

He broke away, stroking her cheek and throat. "I have a plane to catch. I love you, Faith.''

A knot filled her throat and she was afraid if she spoke she would cry. She watched him pick up Merry. He paused and looked at her. "If you leave, what will you do with Merry? You can't take her with you.''

"You know I'll take care of her until you're back, but then I'm gone.''

"I hope not,'' he said solemnly. He hugged and kissed Merry, then he handed the baby to Faith, picked up his carry-on and draped his arm across Faith's shoulders. "I'll call you tonight.''

At the door, Jared leaned over Merry to kiss Faith again, a long, slow, lingering kiss that was heartbreaking.

He strode to his pickup, a long-legged, jeans-clad cowboy, and she felt as if he were tearing her heart out and taking it with him. She waved, telling Merry to wave bye-bye. Merry's small hand waved in the air.

"That's right, love. Daddy's gone bye-bye," Faith said, letting the tears fall now. "I love you," she added.

Jared would be gone nine days, and Faith knew she had some tough decisions to make.

On the fifth day she missed her period. Two days later, she called Meg and asked her sister if she could move in with her temporarily.

"Of course you can move in here," Meg said quietly. "I thought you said Jared is gone."

"He is. I told him if he left, I wouldn't be here when he came back."

"You're sure about what you're doing?"

"I think so," Faith said, wondering whether she was sure about anything any longer.

"What about Merry?"

"Can I bring her with me until he gets back and can take her?"

"You know you can."

"I can take her to Mom's when I'm at work. I've already talked to her about it."

"Don't be ridiculous. It's summer, and the kids are home. What's one more kid around here, and the girls adore playing with her. When are you coming?"

"I need to pack and then I'll be over."

"Does he know this?"

"Yes, he does," Faith said, thinking about the hours they had spent on the phone since he left.

"It seemed like you were pretty happy."

"I was, but there are problems."

"Okay. See you when we see you."

Faith replaced the receiver and hot tears gushed, falling over her hands. She didn't want to leave Jared, but she couldn't stay. And she might be taking a baby of her own away with her. She felt her flat stomach. She was only two days late, but she had never been late in her life.

She heard Merry cry and she turned around to hurry to her room.

The last thing she did before leaving was prop a note to him on the kitchen table. She looked around the room that was filled with memories that tore at her. She couldn't stay and she couldn't go. With tears in her eyes she turned and went out the back door, locking it behind her. She had already packed her car with their bags.

Merry began to cry, fussing again as if Faith's unhappiness was jarring her small system, too.

"Don't start crying, sweetie, or I'll cry right along with you," Faith said, jiggling Merry and then settling her into her car seat and buckling it.

She slid behind the wheel and started the motor, looking at the house once more and seeing only a tall, lean cowboy.

Two days later Jared unlocked the back door and entered the kitchen. The moment he saw the note propped on the kitchen table, his heart lurched.

A week later, Jared sat on horseback and surveyed his land. He'd known he was going to miss Faith dreadfully, but he couldn't have imagined the all-consuming pain that had eaten at him for the past week. How many times had he picked up a receiver to call her and tell her to come back, that he would never ride in a rodeo again. But he'd stopped because he needed this year's earnings for the ranch to survive. And he prayed constantly that she might change her mind, but the more time that passed, the more he gave up that idea. He had a nanny for Merry, Mrs. Slocum, a nice woman with high recommendations who had agreed to live on the ranch. He had bought a trailer house and had it brought near the main house.

"Dammit," he swore softly, turning the horse, trying to get his mind back on cattle when all he could see was Faith's big green eyes, remember her soft cries of passion, dream about loving her again. "I miss you so damned much," he said to no one, wishing the wind could sweep the words right to her heart. And he knew if he didn't get her out of his thoughts, he was going to get hurt riding because he was no longer concentrating as he should. "Faith, darlin', how I need you! And so does Merry." Merry had been fussy ever since Faith left. His little Merry who had always been smiles and sunshine. Maybe she was picking up on his unhappiness. Whatever it was, she had lost her constant sunny disposition. "Darlin' Faith," he whispered again, looking longingly over his shoulder at the hill in the distance where they had made love for the first time.

That same morning, Faith sped through traffic on the freeway, heading downtown to work, her thoughts on Jared and Merry. She slowed for a red light, then glanced at her watch. Jared would already be up and working. They had talked once since his return a week ago and it ended in a stalemate. And though their marriage was on shaky ground, Jared had made it clear she could see Merry whenever she wanted. She knew he had a nanny now, and that he had moved to the ranch.

She had never dreamed she could miss him so badly. And instead of the ache and longing fading, they intensified.

And the nights. Nights were horrible, lonely, unbearable. She'd lived with Meg for four days and then found a furnished apartment that she had no interest in and hated to go home to. Her life had dulled to empty days and sleepless nights.

The green light flashed and Faith accelerated. Suddenly a car whipped through the intersection, running the red light, and Faith saw it only a second before it broadsided her car and spun her across the intersection. Her car struck another car, and she hit her head, darkness exploding as she lost consciousness.

Faith could hear someone calling to her. Sirens blared and as she tried to get out of the car, she felt disoriented, uncertain. Then she remembered the car and the crash. She climbed out on the passenger side, and someone thrust a handkerchief in her hand.

"Here, miss. Your head is bleeding."

She had been unaware of the blood and pressed the clean white handkerchief against her temple. The tall, brown-haired man held out a card. "If you need a witness, here's my number. I saw the guy run the red light. I have a cellular phone if you need to call your work."

While she thanked him, a police car arrived and in minutes she was surrounded by police, a paramedic and witnesses. She called work to explain what had happened and then called her mother to tell her she was fine in case the accident came over the news. Then she called Alice, who said she would come pick her up.

It was over an hour later when she got back to her apartment, washed and changed. The cut on her temple was not as bad as she had first feared. Alice had driven to the crash to get her, and now Faith had Alice's car for the rest of the day, yet she wasn't going back to work. She stood at the window of her apartment, but saw nothing outside.

Instead, she was remembering Jared telling her she faced danger when she drove to work as much as he did with his bull riding. She was gripped with fear when she watched him ride, but that wildness in him was what had drawn her to him in the first place.

Jared was right. Life was filled with risk. And it was too precious to live wrapped up in fear. Tomorrow morning she had a doctor's appointment, and then she would know whether or not she was pregnant. Although she was certain what the answer would be.

She looked at the apartment that held no memories, no loving or laughter, no scrape of boots on the floor or babble of a baby. Was this what she wanted? Never!

Her pulse jumped at the thought of Merry and Jared. They were worth all sorts of risks. Since Jared had come into her life, it had been filled with joy and excitement.

"Jared," she whispered, glancing through the doorway at the phone in the kitchen. "Jared, you were right," she whispered.

Twelve

She was pregnant! Oblivious to the summer downpour, she walked out of her doctor's office. She wanted to leap in the air with joy. And she wanted to rush to find Jared and tell him. She stopped, forgetting she was standing in the rain beside a tall building on a busy thoroughfare. The city faded from her consciousness. All she could think of was Jared. They were going to have a baby!

Dazed, she walked to her car, closed her umbrella and slid behind the wheel, sitting, staring at the raindrops as they streamed down the windshield. She placed her hand on her stomach. They were going to have a baby. *She* was going to have a baby. This was what she'd wanted when she entered into their marriage. And in the back of her mind, all along, she had thought if she had a baby, she would be complete. When she married, she had felt if she didn't fall in love with Jared and things didn't work out, she could leave him and raise her baby by herself and be completely happy. But she knew she could never be happy without her husband, and the little girl they already had. She felt a wrenching ache to tell Jared the news.

Faith was supposed to return to work. Instead, she drove to the house on Peoria. She still had her key and she entered through the back door. The house was silent, empty, yet every room was filled with Jared's presence as memories stormed her. He had moved some of the furniture to the ranch, and there were bare places where there once had been tables and chairs.

She went upstairs and stood in the doorway of the bedroom. Their big bed was gone. Drawers were open, the closet doors stood open. He had moved everything to the ranch.

Memories swirled—moments in his arms, intimate moments of passion in bed. She crossed the room to the phone, which was on the floor. Wondering whether he had disconnected it, she picked it up and heard a hum.

She wondered whether she had made the most colossal mistake. She remembered how impetuous he was; how much women flirted with him. Suppose someone else was already moving into his life?

And the most crucial question of all: could she put up with his bull riding? She was going to have to. She just prayed it wasn't too late to try to get back what she had thrown away by leaving him.

Call him, an inner voice urged. *Go back to him.*

Her hand paused briefly over the phone, and then she knew with glaring certainty she didn't want to wait anymore. This was one time in her life she wasn't going to be cautious. She was going to act as swiftly and impulsively as Jared. She picked up the phone and called the ranch, listening to rings, her heart pounding with eagerness.

"I love you," she whispered. "Please pick up the phone so I can tell you."

Instead, she heard Jared's bass voice as the answering machine clicked on. She replaced the receiver. She didn't want to leave a message—she had to talk to him to tell him she was coming home.

Home. Merry. Jared. Faith placed her hand on her stomach. She ached to be in Jared's arms, to hold him and tell him that she loved him, absolutely, completely and without stipulations.

She called out of work. Rain still came down in a steady stream, and she stared at the shimmering sheets on the windowpanes as she called the ranch again. This time she left a message, then hung up the receiver. She drove to her apartment to pack.

She would stop by the office on the way out of town. It would take about an hour to wind up things there and to tell them she would not be in tomorrow, either.

Her pulse hummed with eager anticipation. Jared. She would see him soon. If he was out of town, she would wait. She loved the man, and she was going home to him. They were still married and she wanted it to work out. She was going to do her best to see that it did. And they had a baby on the way.

"Here I come, mister, whether you're ready or not!" she said as she locked the door behind her.

Half an hour later, dressed in jeans and a long-sleeved Western shirt, she stopped at the office, but was delayed while Porter piled papers in front of her and her secretary gave her calls.

Jared climbed out of the muddy pickup and slammed the door. He had taken Merry to Mrs. Slocum's this morning because of the rain and mud. He could get Merry to the older woman's house easier than she could get out to his. Now the sun was trying to come out, the earth was steaming, and water dripped from every leaf and eave.

He was covered in mud and had spent the morning repairing a fence that went down in the night. He peeled off his boots on the back porch, dropped his coat and tossed his hat down on a chair before he unlocked the back door and went inside.

The silence of the house always reminded him of his loss. He missed Faith more than ever—something he intended to change this weekend.

He saw the blinking light on the answering machine and crossed the room to play back the messages.

The first was from the hardware store in Coweta, saying that the baling wire he had ordered was in and ready to be picked up. The second call was from Faith. His heart lurched at the sound of her voice, and he leaned closer to the machine as if he could get closer to her.

"Jared, sorry I missed you. This is Monday morning. I don't know where you and Merry are. I'm going by the office for an hour and around ten o'clock, I'll head to the ranch. We need to talk," she said, her voice filled with emotion, and he wondered whether or not she was crying.

"Ahh, darlin'." He glanced at the clock. It was one o'clock. If she'd gone to the office at ten, she should be at the ranch by—

His thoughts lurched. *The bridge.* The bridge leading to the ranch that was usually over a bone-dry creek bed was now unsafe to cross.

"Dammit!" He ran for the back door. Last week they had had a torrential rain and it had weakened the structure. He had started to repair it, but then the rain commenced again and he had to wait. He had placed a sign beside the road warning anybody that it wasn't safe, but the storms ast night and this morning could have demolished his sign.

He hopped on one foot, pulling on a boot and then pulling on the other. Dashing across the yard, he jammed his at on his head. He raced to his pickup, jumped in and urned on the engine. He started down the road, swearing ach time the pickup skidded in muddy, slick ruts.

Leaning over the wheel, he drove as fast and recklessly s he dared. "Don't cross the bridge, Faith! Don't cross !" He yanked up the cellular phone and punched her office number, praying she was still there and had been detained. Visions of the raging creek danced in his mind. It would now be up and roaring.

The sun was shining, but he knew it hadn't been long enough since the deluge for the water to have gone down.

"Graphic Design," a cheerful voice answered, and he tried to remember the receptionist's name, only able to see her bright blue eyes and red hair.

"Emily, is Faith in? This is her husband."

"Sorry, Mr. Whitewolf, she left a long time ago. She won't be back for a few days."

He swore, his heart and stomach knotting. "How long ago did she leave? It's important that I know exactly."

"Oh, gee. I think she's been gone since almost twelve o'clock."

"Thanks," he said tersely, and clicked off, tossing the phone down in the seat beside him. He glanced at his watch and his insides tightened another notch. By now she would have reached the bridge.

He prayed, slipping and slowing, knowing he would be no help to Faith if he slid and got stuck in the mud. Whenever he could, he accelerated, racing across the ranch. He was almost to the bridge, his palms were sweaty, his heart thudding. He topped a hill and his breathing stopped.

Faith's black car was already on the bridge.

Thirteen

Faith turned at a bend in the road. Her gaze swept the landscape for any sign of Jared. The day was crystal clear after the rain, the land still green and lush, wildflowers blooming with tall yellow sunflowers scattered across the fields. The sun was high, lifting her spirits even higher, if that was possible. She would see him soon. And she wasn't leaving him this time.

She followed another curve and drew her breath as she started downhill, braking to avoid getting stuck. Mud was deep and the car slipped, but she barely noticed. Her attention was riveted on the tumbling waters ahead. The creek bed had always been dry. Jared had said it could fill and now it had.

A gushing torrent of water rushed along only inches below the bridge. A board was nailed to a tree. Whatever writing had been on it was now runny, and she gave it little notice because all her attention was on the roaring creek that looked like a river. She had to cross it or go back to the city.

She debated only a minute. The water was still below the bridge, not over it. She slowed, and every foot nearer she felt greater trepidation about driving across the bridge. She remembered how it rattled and shook when there was no water. She reached it and started across. It shook and she could feel it sway, but she was on it now and there was no going back. The swaying increased. A loud crack sounded like a gunshot.

Faith watched in horror as the end of the bridge seemed to sway and then tumble away into the water.

The car was going down. She was going to wash away.

Her mind raced and she opened the window, unsnapping her seat belt and trying to get out of the car. She got her head and shoulders through, trying to fling herself out of the window. Cold water poured over her.

"Faith!"

The call sounded like Jared's voice, but she couldn't think about anything except survival. Cold water swamped her, taking her down, the current tumbling her along. She gagged and closed her mouth, struggling to reach the surface. Water flung her against something solid, and pain burst in her shoulder. She kept fighting to reach the top. Her lungs felt as if they would burst and then she broke through, gulping air.

"Faith!"

It was him. "Help!" She couldn't fight the current and was swept along. She struggled, trying to reach a bank. The water pulled her under again and then she broke the surface, gulping for air, fighting with all her strength to move to the bank.

Strong arms closed around her suddenly. "The baby!" she screamed over the roar of the water.

"She's okay!" Jared yelled back. They were both borne on the current, and she struggled along with him, but to no avail. Ahead, a large log bobbed and floated and a new terror gripped her. If they slammed into the log—

Her stomach instinctively tightened, and she renewed her effort to cross the rush of water bearing them downstream.

And she realized they were beginning to move out of the middle of the stream. The bank loomed closer, but they were nearing the log that disappeared below the surface. She wanted to double over and protect her stomach, protect their baby, but she couldn't and still stay afloat.

"The baby!" she cried again, terrified they would hit the submerged log.

"She's all right!" Jared yelled back, and turned them in the opposite direction.

"Jared, the bank—" She screamed above the constant roar of tumbling water. And then she saw why he was turning her. Ahead, a tree had fallen into the water. If they were swept into it, he would hit it first.

She prayed the log was nowhere near them, and then it bobbed to the surface only yards ahead of them. She looked at the tree rushing up to meet them.

"Hang on," he yelled. "Put your arms around me."

She wrapped her arms around his chest and then jammed against his body, her legs sucked in an undertow, but they were against the tree. She caught a branch and released him as they both worked their way toward the bank. Jared held her, his arm around her waist. She waded in deep mud that sucked her down and pulled on her legs and feet. And then they were out of the water and she fell into his arms.

"I love you!" she cried, sobbing and shaken now that the ordeal was over.

He picked her up and strode up the hill, carrying her back along the creek toward the road. She clung to him, gasping for breath. "I can walk."

"I'm not letting go of you," he said gruffly, and his arms tightened around her. She raised her mouth for his kiss. His pickup was standing in the road, door thrown open, motor still running.

He reached in, turned off the motor and set her on her feet. Faith looked up into his dark eyes and then he swept her to him, his arms crushing her against his chest as he leaned down to kiss her. She felt faint, her heart pounding and her insides in a free fall. When he raised his head, his dark eyes bore into her.

"I put a sign up, warning everyone not to get on the bridge."

She glanced across the roaring water and remembered the sign she had barely given a glance. "I was too busy looking at the creek."

"Let's go home," he said. He got the blanket out of the pickup and handed it to her, and she wrapped herself in it while he retrieved the boots that he had yanked off before going in the creek after her. He threw them on the floor of the pickup and pulled her close beside him. She wrapped her arms around his waist and clung to him.

"Merry is at Mrs. Slocum's house. I'll call her and ask her to keep Merry until I come get her tonight." Jared tightened his arm around her. He didn't know why she had come out to the ranch, but whatever the reason, he hoped he could keep her there. When he had watched her go into the creek, he felt as if he were being torn in two. He wanted to love and hold her all night long. And he was scared to hope she had come back for good.

As soon as he slowed and parked by the back door, he climbed out and reached for her. A rainbow arced across the sky over them, soft tints against a deep blue sky, but it was nothing compared to the rainbow of hope in his heart. He led her inside, closed and locked the door and looked down at her.

"Let me call Mrs. Slocum so we won't have any interruptions."

"All right, but sometime tonight, bring Merry home. I haven't seen her in a long time. I missed you both."

He gave Faith a quick hug and then he crossed the kitchen, tracking mud, and picked up the phone.

Faith had lost her sneakers in the muddy creek. She stood, still dripping slightly, and took in the sight of him. His jeans were muddy to his thighs, and his T-shirt was plastered to his body, every sculpted muscle clearly revealed. She loved him, bull riding and all. She dropped the blanket and began to unfasten her jeans.

He replaced the receiver, his midnight eyes filled with fires that sent flames soaring in her. He reached out to draw her to him.

"I don't care whether you ride bulls or not," she told him. "I need you."

"God, I missed you," he said softly, and pulled her to him to kiss her.

It was almost two hours later that she lay in his arms in bed, warm, dry, exhausted from loving and showering together and loving again. She sat up cross-legged, pulling a sheet up and tucking it under her arms.

He looked amused, one corner of his mouth curving slightly. "Why the sudden modesty?"

"I want your undivided attention."

"I can show you how to get my undivided attention," he said, tugging at the sheet and running his finger along the curve of a breast.

"Will you listen to me?" she said, tingling with excitement, wanting to tell him her news.

"Of course," he said attentively, but his fingers still strayed languidly over her.

"Jared," she said, catching his hand and holding it.

"I'm listening, darlin'. Say what you have to say."

"I don't care if you ride in rodeos."

"Thank you," he said solemnly. "But I *do* care how you feel…so I'm giving up the bulls after this season."

"Jared, I never meant for you to give up a dream. I just care about you so much. And I wanted you to know that I realize now life—and love—are gambles, and I don't want to waste a single, precious moment with you. I'm back to stay."

"That, darlin', is the best news I've heard since you agreed to marry me. Now, come here and let's seal it with a kiss."

"You stay right there," she said, pushing him back against the pillow as he started to sit up.

"There's more?" he asked.

"There's a lot more. Want me to tell you what you'll be doing next Memorial Day weekend?"

"Sure, darlin'." He lay back against the pillows with his hands behind his head. His skin was brown, smooth and warm, and his dark eyes were filled with satisfaction and love. "What will we be doing? You look like the dog that ate the Thanksgiving turkey."

"I'm waiting for it to dawn on you."

"Now I am curious. Next May..." Suddenly he sat up, sweeping her into his arms. "Tell me, woman, or I'll kiss you until I get the truth out of you."

She stroked his jaw. "We're going to have another baby!"

His smile vanished, and the look in his eyes made tears spring to her eyes. He pulled her to him to hug her and then he kissed her, finally moving back to look at her again. "That's why you came back," he said solemnly.

"I came back because I love you."

Jared's heart felt as if it would burst with joy as he heard her declaration. She was back and now they would truly have a home and a family. "Ah, darlin'! I adore you."

"And I've given notice at work, Jared," she said. "I know you're in a financial crunch now with starting the ranch. And I intend to work freelance from here sometimes, but right now, I feel like Merry needs a mommy and, of course, our baby will need me to stay fit and healthy. I told them I'd stay until they get someone, and that might take a little while, but not long."

"You're sure?" he asked quietly. "Because I don't want you to give up your dream."

She nodded, running her hands over his shoulder. "I'm very sure."

"I love you, Faith." He gazed into her eyes, and she felt encompassed in a velvet darkness that was filled with love. "I've always loved you from that first moment you came bustin' through the bushes and rescued us. Welcome home, darlin'," he whispered, and returned to kissing her.

Faith wound her arms around his neck, joyful to be back in his arms, knowing she had come home for good.

Epilogue

Faith rocked steadily as she looked at their six-month-old daughter sleeping in her arms. Her gaze swung from little Steffie to Jared who sat across the room reading to Merry.

As he finished the story about a family of rabbits, his gaze lifted and met Faith's. Warmth filled her at the love she saw in his eyes.

"Now, sweetie, it is bedtime," he said to Merry.

"Mommy," Merry said, sliding off her father's lap and hurrying across the family room to Faith. Merry was already bathed and ready for bed in her bunny-covered pink pajamas, her silky black hair curling over her shoulders.

She leaned against Faith's knee and touched Stephanie's cheek. "Sissy sleep?"

"Yes, she's asleep."

"Which you are going to be soon, my little one," Jared said, swinging her up into his arms. Merry giggled as she wrapped her arms around his neck. Faith looked up at them both and smiled. Her tall, lean cowboy husband was a very good father, and she knew she would never have the time for even the small bit of free-lance work she did from the ranch if he weren't so caring with the little girls.

Holding the sleeping baby close in her arms, Faith stood and walked beside them as they headed toward the nursery where Merry kissed her baby sister on the cheek before Faith placed the baby in her crib.

Then the three of them went to Merry's pink-and-white bedroom where Faith turned down the comforter on the four-poster bed, shoving stuffed bears aside. Merry rescued them, piling them around her as she settled against the white sheets. Merry pulled a battered stuffed horse into her arms, cuddling it and patting the bed beside her. "Story, Mommy."

Faith sat where her daughter indicated and Merry patted the space on her other side. "Daddy."

Jared stretched out beside their daughter, pulling her into his arms while Faith told the story of the three bears. Faith looked at Merry with her rosy cheeks and dark hair and lashes. She looked soft and sweet curled against Jared. He was rumpled, still in jeans and a chambray shirt from his day's work.

Before the end of the story, Merry's eyes were closed and Jared gently extracted himself and tucked the covers around her. He came around the bed to join Faith, draping his arms across her shoulders as they made to leave Merry's room.

"We're lucky," Faith said as she switched out the light. "We have beautiful little girls."

"All three of my girls are beautiful, and I'm the luckiest guy on earth," Jared said quietly. She turned to head back to the family room, but he tightened his arm around her shoulders. "Come here."

"*We're* lucky," she repeated softly, thinking how well he was doing with his saddle bronc riding and how the ranch was thriving. And he had seemed completely willing to give up the bull riding.

He led her into their big bedroom and closed the door quietly, leaning against it and pulling her into his arms to smile at her. "I love you, darlin'."

Filled with happiness, Faith brushed her fingers over his jaw, touching the rough stubble. "I love you, too, cowboy. Little did I know when I rushed through the spirea bushes at the park what I was getting myself into."

"You were an angel of mercy come to our rescue."

"I doubt if you needed much rescuing. You would have taken care of Merry if I hadn't been there."

"Not so. I needed you badly and I always will." He pulled her closer, and she wrapped her arms around his waist, smelling the familiar scents of horses and cotton.

"You were right about a lot of things," she said. "I was ready for more in my life. So much more," she said, thinking about their life together, the girls, the home she loved. "This house did fix up."

"Well, you were right yourself," he said, kissing her ear, pushing away her cotton blouse to nuzzle her neck. "I'm damned glad to be done with bull riding. In those eight seconds your whole life flashes before you sometimes."

"You never told me that before!" she said, and he chuckled softly, looking at her tenderly. And then the moment changed and she saw the fires burn in his dark eyes as he became solemn.

"I need you, darlin', more than the air I breathe," he said in a husky voice. He leaned down to trail kisses along her throat while his hand slid over her ribs.

"I couldn't resist you then, cowboy. I don't want to resist you now," she whispered as she turned her head, pulling his head down and placing her lips on his. Jared tightened his arms around her and Faith clung to him, knowing that day in the park had started her on a lifetime of love.

* * * * *

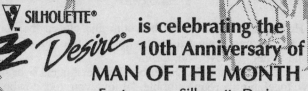
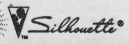

If you enjoyed what you just read,
then we've got an offer you can't resist!

Take 2 bestselling love stories FREE!

Plus get a FREE surprise gift!

Clip this page and mail it to Silhouette Reader Service™

IN U.S.A.	IN CANADA
3010 Walden Ave.	P.O. Box 609
P.O. Box 1867	Fort Erie, Ontario
Buffalo, N.Y. 14240-1867	L2A 5X3

YES! Please send me 2 free Silhouette Desire® novels and my free surprise gift. Then send me 6 brand-new novels every month, which I will receive months before they're available in stores. In the U.S.A., bill me at the bargain price of $3.12 plus 25¢ delivery per book and applicable sales tax, if any*. In Canada, bill me at the bargain price of $3.49 plus 25¢ delivery per book and applicable taxes**. That's the complete price and a savings of over 10% off the cover prices—what a great deal! I understand that accepting the 2 free books and gift places me under no obligation ever to buy any books. I can always return a shipment and cancel at any time. Even if I never buy another book from Silhouette, the 2 free books and gift are mine to keep forever. So why not take us up on our invitation. You'll be glad you did!

225 SEN CNFA
326 SEN CNFC

Name	(PLEASE PRINT)	
Address	Apt.#	
City	State/Prov.	Zip/Postal Code

* Terms and prices subject to change without notice. Sales tax applicable in N.Y.
** Canadian residents will be charged applicable provincial taxes and GST.
   All orders subject to approval. Offer limited to one per household.
   ® are registered trademarks of Harlequin Enterprises Limited.

DES99   ©1998 Harlequin Enterprises Limited

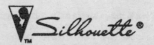

Bestselling author

LINDSAY McKENNA

continues the drama and adventure of her
popular series with an all-new, longer-length
single-title romance:

MORGAN'S MERCENARIES

HEART OF THE JAGUAR

Major Mike Houston and Dr. Ann Parsons were in the heat
of the jungle, deep in enemy territory. She knew Mike's
warrior blood kept him from the life—and the love—he
silently craved. And now she had so much more at stake.
For the beautiful doctor carried a child. His child...

Available in January 1999, at your favorite retail outlet!

Look for more **MORGAN'S MERCENARIES** in 1999,
as the excitement continues in the Special Edition line!

Silhouette®

PSMORGMERC

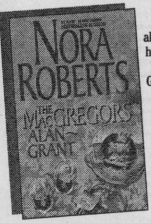

SILHOUETTE® Desire®

COMING NEXT MONTH

#1195 A KNIGHT IN RUSTY ARMOR—Dixie Browning
Man of the Month/The Lawless Heirs
When Travis Holiday found out he had a son, he realized it was time to settle down—no more heroics! Then a long-haired goddess named Ruanna Roberts was stranded in a storm, and Travis just had to save her. But Ruanna was determined to rescue *Travis!* Could she crumble the armor around his soul and claim his heart for her own…?

#1196 SOCIETY BRIDE—Elizabeth Bevarly
Fortune's Children: The Brides
Weeks away from a business marriage and Rene Riley was secluded on a remote ranch with the man of her dreams! Though cowboy Garrett Fortune defined unbridled passion, Rene was the only woman he wanted. He just had to convince her that the only *partnership* she was going to enter into was a marriage to him!

#1197 DEDICATED TO DEIRDRE—Anne Marie Winston
Butler County Brides
Ronan Sullivan and Deirdre Patten hadn't seen one another for years, but one look and Deirdre knew the desire was still there. Ronan needed a place to stay, and Deirdre had a room to rent. But opening her home—and heart—to Ronan could prove very perilous indeed.…

#1198 THE OUTLAW JESSE JAMES—Cindy Gerard
Outlaw Hearts
Rodeo was the only mistress in cowboy Jesse James's life. He liked slow, hot seductions and short, fast goodbyes. Then Sloan Gantry sashayed into his life. Could this sweet temptress convince the "outlaw" that the only place to run was straight into her arms…?

#1199 SECRET DAD—Raye Morgan
Single mom Charlie Smith would do anything for her child—even marry rugged mercenary Denver McCaine. She now had his protection, but Charlie was wondering how much tender affection one woman could take before dreams of happily-ever-after took hold of her wistful heart.…

#1200 LITTLE MISS INNOCENT?—Lori Foster
No matter what he did, Dr. Daniel Sawyer could not shake his desire for Lace McGee. The sweet seductress had a tempting mouth and a will of iron. But there was also uncertainty in Lace's eyes. Was it there to drive him away—or did she hide an innocence he had never suspected?